Marked by Honor

Knights Of Honor

Book Two

Alexa Aston

Copyright © 2017 by Alexa Aston
Print Edition

Published by Dragonblade Publishing, an imprint of Kathryn Le Veque Novels, Inc

All rights reserved. No part of this book may be used or reproduced in any manner whatsoever without written permission, except in the case of brief quotations embodied in critical articles or reviews.

Table of Contents

Chapter One 1
Chapter Two 9
Chapter Three 19
Chapter Four 25
Chapter Five 31
Chapter Six 38
Chapter Seven 47
Chapter Eight 54
Chapter Nine 64
Chapter Ten 71
Chapter Eleven 80
Chapter Twelve 88
Chapter Thirteen 98
Chapter Fourteen 106
Chapter Fifteen 112
Chapter Sixteen 119
Chapter Seventeen 126
Chapter Eighteen 135
Chapter Nineteen 142
Chapter Twenty 150
Chapter Twenty-One 158
Chapter Twenty-Two 167
Chapter Twenty-Three 176

Chapter Twenty-Four 184
Chapter Twenty-Five 191
Epilogue 202
About the Author 205

CHAPTER ONE

Southern England—1363

SHE COULDN'T WAIT to ride again. She pulled free of her mother's hand and raced across the meadow. Warm summer sun caressed her back. Blaze galloped through the green grass, carrying her father. She ran in his direction as fast as her legs would carry her.

He spotted her and smiled, turning the horse toward her. She knew what to do next. Standing as still as she could, she held her arms wide. The beating hooves came her way as she held her breath. Her father scooped her up in one swift motion, seating her in front of him. The scent of leather and horse swirled in the air as his arms encircled her. She loved being close to him. He was a bear of a man who became gentle as a lamb whenever near his daughter or wife.

"Go fast," she demanded.

As always, the horse responded to her father's wordless commands. Blaze took off full speed. She squealed in delight as the wind whipped her hair about. From up high, she could see the castle in the distance and all their surrounding land.

They flashed past her waving mother. The world became a blur of colors as the horse went faster and faster.

Her father's laughter came from deep within his belly, filling the air around her. She joined in, delighted to spend this special time together. As he gazed down at her with adoration and love, she knew she was his special girl. Then Blaze stumbled.

Suddenly, she was sailing through the air like a bird. Her father gripped her tightly, but his expression scared her. He managed to twist them around before they hit the ground hard. Fear rippled through her as she hovered above her father, knowing he'd intentionally cushioned her fall. She wanted to cry but couldn't. It was too hard to suck in a full breath. When she was finally able to breathe, her father's strong arms fell away, releasing her. She rolled to her side and curled into a ball, trembling—frightened to look at him again.

A loud shriek sounded and her mother ran toward them. Falling to her knees, her mother ripped at her hair. Did her mother blame her for the accident? She pushed herself into a sitting position and glanced over at her father. His head rested in an unnatural position, but their eyes met momentarily and she could see the panic in them. Fear spiked inside her again. Couldn't he get up? The light in his eyes faded.

She screamed.

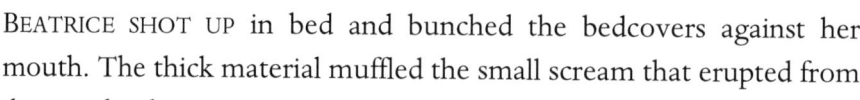

BEATRICE SHOT UP in bed and bunched the bedcovers against her mouth. The thick material muffled the small scream that erupted from deep within her.

She fell back against the pillows. Every time she awakened from a nightmare, her body was drenched with sweat. She tried to relax, but the knot in her stomach ached. She forced herself to breathe slowly. Finally, the last remnants of horror began to fade.

She pushed away the thoughts of her father and the last time they were together. It did no good to think about him. He'd been gone ten and seven years, and her life had changed drastically.

Beatrice tossed aside the covers and swung her legs to the floor. They still shook, so she didn't trust standing just yet. Instead, she focused on the day ahead. A day which would be like yesterday. And the one that came tomorrow.

Every day blended together, from tending to her mother's needs to mending, washing, and cooking. If it was a good day, her mother wouldn't be ill-tempered. She would listen quietly as Beatrice played her a few songs on the lute. Hopefully, her mother would manage to eat something without vomiting it back up and then nap for the remainder of the day. Only then would Beatrice get most of the household work done.

Once evening came, she looked forward to the time spent with her grandfather, who would share stories of the past about his own life and England's glory. Often, they played several games of tables or read together from the Bible before their nightly prayers.

Beatrice wondered how different life might have been if her father had lived. Or if her mother had been able to have more children—especially an heir. Instead, she grew up in her grandfather's rented manor house with no luxuries, isolated from children her own age. As the years passed, her mother lost the will to live and gradually became bedridden. Beatrice became responsible for keeping their small household running and she'd learned to make what little they had last. Life had gone on this way for many years, but now her grandfather's health was in question.

She pushed that thought aside, not wanting to deal with it, and dressed for the day in her smock and kirtle. Beatrice unbound the straight, dark brown hair which fell to her waist and combed through it before braiding it again in a single plait. Now ready for the day, she stirred the embers of the kitchen fire and fed more wood into it before going outside to gather eggs from their two hens. After completing those tasks, she joined her grandfather for their morning devotional. The old man already knelt in prayer, his head bowed and gnarled hands wrapped around one another. She joined in the Latin that he'd taught her, the words flowing easily after so many years of practice. As she spoke, she stole a glance at him.

Over the years, his thick thatch of hair had turned white, but these days Beatrice worried about his trembling hands. Twice this week he'd lost his balance and stumbled into the furniture. Though she'd voiced her concerns, he shrugged them off, saying that she worried too much.

Their prayers came to a close. Beatrice rose and grasped his arm in order to help him stand. She released her hold on him once he seemed steady on his feet. He rewarded her with a sweet, knowing smile. For a moment, she caught a glimpse of her mother in that smile and it tugged at her heart.

"Shall we break our fast, Granddaughter?" He offered her his arm.

She slipped her hand through the crook and led them to the kitchen, glad that he allowed her to help support him. As he took a seat at the small wooden table, she pulled out the bread she had baked yesterday afternoon and retrieved some cool ale for them to drink.

"Have we any raspberry jam?" he asked hopefully.

"For you and your sweet tooth? Always." Bringing the crock to the table, she watched him liberally smear his bread with the fruit preserve.

They ate in companionable silence, content in one another's company. Beatrice noticed that the tremors seemed worse this morning as he brought the pewter cup to his mouth.

He caught her eye. "We need to talk, child."

His serious tone made her wince. She worried the discussion would involve their lack of coin.

"We talk all the time, Grandfather."

He squeezed her hand. "And I am happy for that. You have been a blessing to me in my old age, Beatrice, though I regret the circumstances that brought you to me. I appreciate you as my blood relative, but you've always been an interesting companion." He paused. "But it's time that we speak of important matters."

Beatrice bit her lip. Somehow, she had a feeling she wouldn't like what he wanted to share with her.

"I know you've been concerned for my health. I am willing to admit that I fear my time draws near."

She protested. "But Grandfather, I—"

"Nay. Let me finish." He took a deep breath. "We must face reality, Beatrice. I need to see you are cared for once I am gone. I have written to my oldest friend about the situation. You've heard me speak of Sir Henry Stollers many times. I hope to hear from him soon."

His words aroused her curiosity. "What might Sir Henry have to do with me, Grandfather?"

He brushed her words aside. "Not now, child. We will speak of the matter once I've received his reply. I only wanted you to know that I am preparing for your future." He rose gingerly from his seat. "Tolly and I are going to hunt this morning while you care for your mother. I hope we'll find good meat to put on our table." He brushed cool lips against her forehead and left the room.

Beatrice pondered his words. He'd spoken of Sir Henry often over the years and how they were the two Henrys who fostered together, inseparable as brothers while they trained as pages, then squires, and, finally, as knights of the realm. Beatrice wondered if her grandfather had asked Sir Henry to make her his ward once he passed.

Because they had no money, no betrothal had been arranged for her. Without a bride price, she'd resigned herself to a life without a husband or children. At two and twenty, she already felt old beyond measure.

Wearily, she washed their mugs and wiped the crumbs from the table. She ladled out some broth that had been warming while they ate and placed it in a bowl before cutting a slice of bread from the loaf and smoothing jam on it. Placing both items on a tray, she took it to her mother's chamber.

Beatrice pushed open the door and brought the tray to the bed. Her mother grew thinner by the day and would probably eat only a few spoonsful of the broth, much less try any of the bread. Beatrice wished now that she hadn't put the jam on it. The bread would only grow soggy—and she knew it would need to be eaten later. Nothing went to waste these days.

"Good morning, Mother." She set the tray down and helped her mother from the bed and to the chamber pot. Arms and legs as thin as twigs poked out from her mother's dressing gown. Beatrice tried not to dwell on her mother's sad appearance as she got her back into the bed.

"I am so tired."

At least Beatrice heard no bitterness in her mother's voice and took that as a good sign. She plumped the pillows and brought her mother to a sitting position.

"Let me feed you some of this broth. I hope you'll try to eat a few bites of the bread, too. Grandfather was especially fond of the jam this morning."

Her mother glanced at the food with disinterest. "I'm not hungry." She closed her eyes.

Should she insist that her mother eat? Beatrice knew it would cause cross words between them if she did, but how was her mother supposed to stay alive when she continually refused every meal?

Before an argument started, her mother started to cough violently. She gasped and wheezed as Beatrice thumped her on the back. As the hacking finally eased, Beatrice was able to feed her mother some of the broth, hoping it might help. Her mother fell back against her pillows in exhaustion.

Beatrice studied the shell of a woman before her. She remembered how breathtakingly beautiful her mother had once been when she was married to her father. Beatrice wished she possessed half of her mother's beauty from the old days. She tenderly stroked her mother's hand as memories flooded her.

"I miss your father."

Startled by her words, Beatrice met her mother's eyes. "I do, too." Her throat constricted. Anytime she thought about him, those last few moments unfolded. He'd sacrificed himself to keep her safe. She could still see her mother drop to her knees next to his still body, weeping as if she would fill the seas with her tears.

"We loved each other so much. I . . . never . . . wanted to look at . . . another."

Had suitors courted her mother after she became a young widow? Beatrice couldn't remember that far into the past since she'd only turned five the day of his death.

She gently squeezed her mother's hand. "I remember that he was a good man." Tears stung her eyes as guilt laced her heart. She always believed she'd caused her father's death and wished it had been she who had died instead. Then her mother would have lived in better health with the man she worshiped by her side. Mayhap they would have had other children—though her mother had lost two babes after Beatrice's birth.

"Oh!" Her mother's eyes widened as she looked across the room, then a smile graced her lips. "I am ready, my love," she said softly.

Beatrice looked over her shoulder, wondering who her mother spoke to.

"Do you see him?" her mother rasped.

Before Beatrice could answer, her mother's fingers tightened painfully around her hand. Then the pressure lessened and her mother's hand fell to the bed as she sighed, not in pain—but in relief. Her eyelids fluttered and closed. The corners of her mouth turned up in a small, secret smile.

Beatrice placed her palm against her mother's cheek. The life had gone from her body. She glanced around the room.

Had her mother actually seen the ghost of her husband?

At least she had been happy at the end. That was what mattered.

Though Beatrice believed that she'd prepared herself for the day her mother would finally pass away, hot tears still poured down her cheeks. She wept as she held her mother's hand for some time, appreciating these last moments together. Sadly, her grandfather had lost his only child, and she had now lost both of her parents. All the death around her made her feel weary.

She heard a noise outside. Going to the small window, she saw Tolly approaching in the distance, driving the cart home from the morning's hunt. She caught sight of a large stag in the back as the servant headed up the pathway. She returned to the bedside and kissed her mother's cheek before she drew the covers over her.

Beatrice went to greet her grandfather, thinking about how to break the sad news to him. When she opened the front door to the manor house, he was nowhere in sight. She stepped out into the sunny day, shielding her eyes with her hand, and saw Tolly scrambling down from the driver's seat.

"Oh, my lady. 'Tis awful." He ran to her, his red eyes brimming with tears. "Sir Henry felled the stag and was so proud. We dragged it to the cart. And then... he cried out. Grabbed at his chest and collapsed. I hurried home as fast as the horse would come. You've got to help him, my lady."

Panic filled Beatrice as she raced to the back of the cart. Her grandfather was stretched out next to the stag. His ashen face made her think that he'd already died. She scrambled into the cart. Relived to feel a weak pulse in his neck, she closed her eyes for a moment.

The sound of her grandfather moving made her open them. He gave her a feeble smile. Beatrice decided not to tell him his daughter had passed. She saw no need to cause senseless heartache when he had so little time left.

"Wait for ... Henry's ... reply. I ... want ... marry ... not worry ..."

"Hush," she told him, stroking his wrinkled cheek. "Save your strength." Beatrice pressed a tender kiss to his forehead. "I love you, Grandfather." Tears rolled down her face.

"Strongbox ..."

She rested her forehead against his, waiting for the dreaded moment he'd take his last breath. Just as she feared ...

Beatrice raised her head. Her mother and grandfather had died within minutes of each other. It was more than she could take. She collapsed against his chest, sobs racking her body as grief swallowed her whole.

CHAPTER TWO

"My lady?"

Beatrice wearily looked up and saw Tolly standing in the doorway. She had just finished washing and dressing both bodies for burial while Tolly dug two side-by-side graves.

"Has the priest come?"

"No, my lady. He should be here soon. But a rider has arrived."

"A rider? What does he want?" They rarely received guests, though they occasionally offered shelter to the few travelers that came their way. Since the manor house was set far from the main road, most passed by, not knowing it was there.

"The man has brought a missive from Sir Henry Stollers." Tolly handed over a rolled parchment with a wax seal.

Sir Henry?

The conversation she'd had with her grandfather only this morning came to mind. This must be the message that he'd anticipated from his friend.

"Ask him to stay in case I need to send a reply. Give him something to eat and drink, Tolly. You know where everything is."

"Aye, my lady. I'll offer him our hospitality and see that his horse is watered and fed."

"Thank you."

Beatrice found her legs suddenly unsteady and took a seat in the wooden chair next to the bed where her grandfather's body lay. She stared at the parchment resting in her lap, not wanting to open it. Too much had already changed in her life today. The contents of this missive could bring even further heartache and transformation.

She broke the seal and unrolled the scroll.

Henry–

I was delighted to hear from you. You've always been the brother of my heart. It has been far too many years since we have seen one another. I can shut my eyes and think back to our younger days, full of swordplay and flirting with pretty young maidens as we walked boldly through life, never backing down from any challenge. I think of you often, my friend, and those times we shared before our lives took such different directions.

Now, as we've grown old, I've missed you even more than I thought possible. Your suggestion of a visit would be a soothing balm to my weary bones. I look forward to meeting this beautiful, intelligent granddaughter of yours and hearing her sing and play the lute. It reminds me of when the two of us thought we could write poetry and set it to song, trying to entice willing women to share kisses with us in darkened alcoves. How I wish we were young again and could live those days over again.

I have a grandson, the only child of Guy, my remaining son. As I write this, Guy is in poor health. It's hard to think that my last surviving child might pass before I do. But my grandson, Edwin, is fine company, handsome and well-spoken, though a bit arrogant at times. I find it one thing to be confident but quite another to be an overconfident braggart. Edwin is only ten and eight, so I hope he will mature before I see my last days since everything will be entrusted to him to continue the Stollers' family legacy.

Edwin is to be married in a few months' time. 'Twould do my heart good to have you and Beatrice come for an extended stay at Brookhaven. You could help us welcome Edwin's bride to our family and celebrate their marriage.

I hope you'll make good on your promise and come to Brookhaven, Henry. I don't think either of us will survive many more summers. I would consider it a pleasure to spend time with my oldest, dearest friend. Please come and stay as long as you can, for you and your granddaughter will always be welcome in my home.

I remain, as always, your loyal and faithful friend.
Henry

Beatrice read the message a second time. She smiled as she finished it, wishing that she and her grandfather could have traveled to Brookhaven together and spent time with Sir Henry.

And then she thought, *Why not?*

She believed that her grandfather had planned to ask Sir Henry to take her on as his ward. It would be impossible to remain at the manor house for long since she hadn't the coin to pay rent. She could travel to Brookhaven and meet with her grandfather's old friend. If he did become her guardian, Beatrice would repay him in many ways. She was quick with a needle and thread and cooked equally well. She could even entertain his guests with her lute playing. If Sir Henry provided her with a home, her worries could be laid to rest.

It concerned her that her grandfather would not be present to act as a bridge between them. If Sir Henry learned of his friend's death, he might rescind his kind invitation. Beatrice knew if he did, she would have nowhere else to go.

Quickly, she pulled out parchment and ink to compose a reply to Sir Henry. She told him that she wrote on her grandfather's behalf, as his hand had a troubling tremor. Since her grandfather had already sent a recent missive to the nobleman, Sir Henry wouldn't be surprised by her words. Promising they would come to Brookhaven in the near future, she left their arrival date open and wrote that they would be there in time to attend the nuptial mass of Edwin Stollers and his bride. Beatrice gambled that once she arrived alone, Sir Henry would prove to be a gracious man and not turn her away.

After the ink had dried, she rolled the small parchment and melted wax to join the ends together before slipping her grandfather's signet ring from his hand in order to seal the missive. She replaced the ring and left the room, making sure to close the door. She didn't want the rider to see inside.

Beatrice hurried to the small kitchen where a lean man with kind eyes greeted her. As she expected, Tolly was nowhere in sight. The shy servant rarely spoke, so she knew he wouldn't have lingered in the kitchen to gossip.

"I am Lady Beatrice Bordel. I hope Tolly saw to your needs?" she asked.

"He did, my lady, and he left to see my horse was taken care of, as well."

She handed him the missive, which he tucked inside his *cotehardie*. "This is from my grandfather. He is resting now, but he asked that I be sure you were treated well before you returned to Sir Henry. May I pack any fresh bread or cheese for you as you make your way home?"

The man nodded. "I would appreciate that, my lady. I have a long ride ahead of me."

His words caused her to ask, "Exactly how long does it take to reach Brookhaven? I'm curious because Sir Henry has asked Grandfather and me to come for an extended visit. He mentioned that we would see his grandson married if we arrived in time."

"I managed to reach here in just over four days' time, but that was by myself and on horseback, setting a brisk pace."

Beatrice drew in a quick breath. Her heart fluttered nervously. "Oh, I can't ride a horse. We'll need to travel to the Stollers' estate by cart."

The courier thought a moment. "It will probably take you almost triple the time, my lady. Mayhap a bit more. The wedding is to take place in about three months, I believe, around the middle of November. I am sure it would please Sir Henry if you could manage to journey to Brookhaven by then. You could stay on through the Christmas holidays." He laughed. "And probably longer. Brookhaven is far to the north and has much harsher weather than your fair southern clime. I'd advise that you stay on till spring to avoid returning on treacherous roads."

"Thank you, sir. I will share this information with my grandfather."

She heard the front door open and Tolly appeared in the kitchen doorway.

"Your horse is ready." He turned and left them.

"A man of few words," the messenger noted.

"That describes Tolly quite well," Beatrice said. "Give me a few minutes to gather things for you."

"I'll await you in the stable," he replied.

She wrapped a chunk of cheese, a loaf of bread, and an entire roasted chicken that had been meant for the next few days' meals. With the stag from this morning's hunt, they would not be in need of meat for a while, so she could afford to be generous.

Beatrice took the food outside and wished the rider a safe journey before she returned to the house. It was time to open the strongbox and see exactly what they had for coin so she could decide her future. Before she reached the door, someone called out from the woods. Turning, she saw the priest making his way toward her.

She would see to her loved ones' burial first—and then find out the state of her grandfather's affairs.

BEATRICE LIFTED THE STRONGBOX from its place in the corner of the room and carried it to the oak table. It was quite heavy, but she'd grown strong from hard work. Her hands lingered above the box. Hesitation would not change what she found inside it, so she inserted the key into the lock. Her grandfather had worn it on a chain around his neck and she had removed it before his burial yesterday.

She pulled out a few bits of parchment, probably letters that had meant something to him. One piece caught her eye when she saw two familiar names. Beatrice skimmed the contents of the page, which turned out to be the betrothal contract between her parents. She gasped at the bride price her grandfather had paid, a vast section of land. Vaguely, she remembered her mother mentioning once that the land had been sold by her father-in-law shortly after the wedding. The sale had added quite a bit of gold to the family coffers.

Setting the contract aside, she counted out twelve pieces of gold nestled at the bottom and stacked them on the table. It was more than she had expected. The money would give her a way to travel to Brookhaven in comfort and not arrive looking destitute. She found her mother's pearl necklace and removed it with care. Beatrice held it up to the light and admired the sheen and size of each pearl. This has been her father's wedding gift to her mother. She kissed the pearls reverently.

Beatrice remembered her parents laughing and dancing, embracing one another with deep love. The clarity of the memories hit her hard. She hadn't known such happy memories existed. Though she appreciated them returning after seeing the necklace, it brought a bitter ache to her soul. Her parents had loved one another so completely.

Something she would never experience.

With trembling fingers, Beatrice opened the clasp and donned the jewelry. She would wear this piece always, in memory of them both. Though the necklace could be sold, she wouldn't part with it for any sum. It was the last link to her parents and the past.

Beatrice glanced about the room and spied their few precious books on a shelf. She could take these with her on the journey to Brookhaven and hopefully find a place to sell them along the way. The furniture all belonged to the manor house. Beyond her few personal possessions, everything else—including the dishes, silver candlesticks, tapestries, and rugs—had come with the rental of the property. Everything she owned would easily fit into a small trunk for her trip north.

Her attention returned to the strongbox. She ran her fingers along the bottom and found the final item, a ruby ring. Tears welled in her eyes. This had been her mother's wedding ring. Beatrice closed her eyes and could picture it on her mother's hand. She opened her eyes and admired the rich color of the jewel set in gold. Her mother must have put it aside after her husband's death, for Beatrice had not seen it in many years. Mayhap the ring had been too painful a reminder of the man her mother had loved and lost.

A sudden movement outside the window caught her eye. Beatrice raced to see who had arrived. It was as she feared.

Amfrid.

Quickly, she pocketed the ring and hurried to the table. She swept all but two of the gold coins from the table and placed them in her deep pocket, along with the key. Beatrice returned two coins and the papers to the chest and quickly took it to its place in the corner under a table. She folded the cloth that rested atop the table back over it, hiding the strongbox from view.

Amfrid knocked at the front door. She answered it since Tolly had gathered their remaining chickens and the goat to take to market to sell as they prepared to leave.

Beatrice took a calming breath and opened the door.

"Good afternoon—"

"I heard of Sir Henry's death." Amfrid pushed past her and strode into the room she had just vacated, having trouble fitting through the narrow doorway.

"Yes, both he and—"

"I am here to collect the rent due." His piggish eyes swept across the room, assessing things.

"I know that Grandfather—"

"Where is the strongbox?" he demanded. "I need my monies immediately."

She fought the bile rising in her throat. Beatrice had never been comfortable in this man's presence, but her grandfather had always acted as a shield whenever Amfrid called upon them.

"I'll fetch it." Her legs felt like lead as she crossed the room and knelt where the strongbox sat. She lifted the cloth.

Amfrid hovered behind her. "I'll get it." He nudged her aside with a booted foot and dragged the strongbox from its place and carried it to the table.

She watched him lick his thick lips greedily as he stared at the strongbox.

"The key. You have it?"

"I do." She eased it from her pocket because she didn't want any of the hidden coins to jingle in her pocket. She handed it to Amfrid and he inserted it into the lock.

His eyes lit with anticipation when he threw back the lid. Beatrice thanked Christ Almighty that she'd had time to conceal most of the coins. If not, the landlord would've taken everything in the box and left her with nothing.

Amfrid tossed the papers aside, scattering them to the floor. He shoved both hands inside and felt around. A deep frown creased his brow. He removed the two gold coins she had placed inside the strongbox.

"This is everything?" he said in dismay. "Surely, he had more."

Beatrice shook her head. "I cannot say. Grandfather never shared his business affairs with me. He only instructed me to be very careful with our household expenses."

He held up a coin in each hand. "I can't believe this is all that Sir Henry had to his name. It barely covers the rent that he owed." Amfrid slipped the coins into his pocket and narrowed his eyes as he studied her. Then his face lit up. "Actually, now that I think upon it, Sir Henry owed me much more than the value of these gold coins."

Suddenly, Beatrice knew what he looked at.

The pearl necklace.

Wild thoughts raced through her head. She would do or say anything to keep this link to her parents.

"I am in the process of closing things up at the manor house. Before his death, Grandfather was going to take me north. To Brookhaven. To . . . to . . . my betrothed," she sputtered. The lie came out before it had fully formed in her thoughts.

Beatrice saw the greedy landlord mull over her words.

She rushed to assure him. "I am sure that if Grandfather left any outstanding debts, my betrothed will make good on them. Let me know how much should be rendered and I'll make sure that you receive payment."

Amfrid took a step toward her and placed his meaty hands upon her shoulders. His fingers tightened till Beatrice almost gasped in pain, but she remained perfectly still.

He brought his face close to hers. His rank breath made her want to flinch, but she stood strong.

"Tell your *betrothed* that I am owed forty, no, fifty pieces of gold."

Her eyes widened. "Surely, you must be mistaken. That amount would cover years of rent."

He glared at her. "I keep careful records. I am never mistaken when it comes to money. I'll expect your intended to pay me. In full." His eyes gleamed. "Until then, I will keep this lovely bit of jewelry to guarantee I receive my payment." He fingered the pearls, the back of his hand resting upon the curve of her breast.

"Please," she pleaded, her eyes filling with tears. "This necklace is the only thing of value that I possess. My father gave it to my mother and she passed it along to me. It has great sentimental value."

Amfrid's fingers returned to her shoulders and dug into her tender flesh. "Take the necklace off," he ordered. He left no room for protest.

She did as he asked, reaching behind her neck and undoing the clasp. As she lowered the necklace, he snatched it from her. He inspected the pearls, looking quite pleased.

Seeing the prized possession in Amfrid's hands caused something to break inside Beatrice. Without fear of the consequences, she plucked the necklace from his fingers.

"You can't have this," she boldly told the landlord. "I told you, my betrothed will make good on any of Grandfather's debts." She held the pearls close to her chest, unwilling to part with the only link she had to her mother.

Shock filled the man's face. His gaze turned threatening. "Woman, give me those pearls now," he warned, "or I'll take them from you."

Beatrice knew he would make good on his threat. There was nothing she could do. Reluctantly, she handed the necklace over to him. She crossed her arms protectively in front of her and took a step back. "Be sure you do not sell them," she said, her tone icy. "I plan to pass these pearls along to my daughter one day."

He snorted. "I won't—as long as I receive payment from your husband-to-be."

She had no way of ever retrieving the necklace. Even if she did, it was far more valuable than what he asked. She realized that, sooner or later, he would sell the necklace for a large profit. Especially when he did not receive word from her.

Amfrid pocketed the jewelry. "I bid you good day." He crossed the room and exited the manor house.

Beatrice slumped to the floor. Angry tears spilled down her cheeks. She brushed them aside, hating that she was a weak woman. A man would never have stood for such behavior. He would have called Amfrid out for his lies, challenging him to fight.

She vowed that she would learn to fight. And somehow, some way, she would acquire the money Amfrid demanded. Beatrice would see that pearl necklace around her neck once more.

Even if it was her last act upon earth.

CHAPTER THREE

Raynor Le Roux gasped. "You stabbed me!" he said in disbelief as he looked down at his opponent.

Alys de Montfort gave him a triumphant smile. "Because *you* weren't paying attention," the child told him. "You taught Ancel and me that focus is the most important part of sparring." She jabbed at him again with the wooden sword in her hand.

This time, he parried, turning aside and pushing against her sword. He knocked it from her hand. Alys scrambled to reclaim it, but Raynor put a booted foot on top of it.

She huffed out a long breath and tapped her foot impatiently. He stifled the laughter that threatened to erupt. Already, Alys resembled her mother, Merryn, in every way, from her tall, lithe frame to her chestnut hair and fiery temperament. Little Alys de Montfort was destined to be a beauty and a handful to the man that claimed her one day.

He retrieved the wooden sword that he'd fashioned for her. She had complained bitterly when he made one for her twin and demanded that he also make one for her—and teach her how to use it. Alys snatched the weapon from his hand.

"It's almost time for me to go," he told her, affectionately brushing a finger down her nose. "Fetch your brother. I'll duel with you both one last time before I leave."

Alys rewarded him with a sweet smile and skipped away.

Raynor's gaze swept over the training yard where Lord Geoffrey de Montfort's knights engaged in practice. Some fought in pairs, wielding swords or maces. Others worked one-on-one with a squire, putting them through their paces.

He would miss Kinwick.

Once, Raynor had hoped it would be his home and that Merryn would become his wife. He fingered the blue garter that he always carried in his pocket. He'd taken it from Merryn's leg the day of her wedding to Geoffrey. But the turn of events in the last several months had written a much different story than the one Raynor had imagined.

His eyes found Geoffrey, who showed a young lad exactly how to wield a heavy bastard sword in two hands. The squire swung it awkwardly. Geoffrey patiently corrected him several times as he showed the boy how to move smoothly with the weapon.

Raynor loved his cousin as a brother. The two had spent their entire boyhoods together, first fostering as pages and squires before they trained to be knights under Sir Lovel. Raynor felt closer to Geoffrey than he did his own brother, Peter, and had stood beside his best friend when he married Merryn Mantel.

And Raynor had searched high and low for Geoffrey when he disappeared the day after he wed.

When Geoffrey failed to turn up, Raynor began to spend more time at Kinwick, watching over Merryn and the twins. He'd fantasized they were his. He loved children and had spent so much time with Ancel and Alys—cheering their first steps, helping them learn to ride—it seemed as if he had sired them.

More importantly, he found himself falling deeply in love with Geoffrey's widow, a woman of considerable intelligence and astounding beauty. Yet, she had only looked upon him as a close friend whom she could depend upon. When a much-changed Geoffrey returned after being gone close to seven years, Raynor had not trusted this stranger. Especially when his comrade refused to reveal where he'd been and why he stayed away from his home for so long.

It took Geoffrey's being secretly imprisoned by Sir Symond Benedict in the Kinwick dungeons and a trip to see King Edward himself before Raynor learned of the plot Lord Berold of Winterbourne had concocted. Only then, did Raynor understand how his cousin had suffered for many years apart from his family, with no hope of ever returning to them.

That nightmare was now in the past with Lord Berold's death. Geoffrey had been freed by Berold's son, Hardwin. After a few months of eating the heavenly meals provided by Kinwick's cook, Geoffrey had gained back his weight and strength. His cousin, once again, walked proudly and had love in his heart.

Though Geoffrey had changed, he'd become an even better man than before. Raynor finally trusted his friend again. Life at Kinwick had returned to normal, and Raynor knew it was time for him to go home to Ashcroft. The recent missive he'd received from Gobert, Ashcroft's steward, implored him to address a multitude of problems that needed his attention.

Alys returned with her twin, and Raynor took on the two of them. Both had learned their lessons well. Each moved with a fluid grace and anticipated his moves.

"There you are!" Merryn called out.

Raynor lowered his weapon, and Ancel and Alys went in for the kill. He spun from their grasp and dropped his own sword as he quickly grabbed each twin around the waist and carried them kicking and swinging over to their mother.

"Stop at once," Merryn commanded, her voice soft but firm.

The children respected her wish. They lowered their weapons and stilled their feet.

"Can you be trusted?" Raynor asked them.

Both nodded, and he set them on the ground.

"Now give me a hug and a kiss, for I need to be on the road."

They protested at first, begging him to stay, but one glance from their mother silenced them. Raynor knelt and gave each a firm embrace. He received kisses from both and promised them he would return to visit as he always had. They retrieved their swords and hurried back to the training yard to engage each other in friendly combat.

"I couldn't find you anywhere," Merryn said. "I was afraid you had left without saying goodbye."

"I told the little ones that we would spar once more before I headed out."

She smiled. "They have enjoyed the swords you made for them. Ancel swears he will be the best prepared page in all of England when he leaves to foster with Hardie."

"He will be. And I had to teach Alys enough clever moves so she could protect herself once she departs for court."

Merryn laughed. "I doubt the queen will allow her to carry around a wooden sword, Raynor."

He grinned. "Mayhap I showed Alys ways to defend herself from ill-mannered court pages without having to use her sword."

Merryn rolled her eyes. "I can see it now. Queen Philippa will send my child home for poking out the eyes of a future duke—or worse. Knowing you, I am sure you taught her to fight dirty."

Raynor shrugged. "Only if a boy grows too familiar with her. Then I gave her permission to kick him in—"

"Enough!" she cried. "I'm sure the king will be highly amused by her antics. The queen, doubtful."

"Alys will excel at court. Ancel, too, will thrive when he leaves to foster at Winterbourne's estate."

Merryn touched his arm. "I will be sorry to see them go. And you, also." She paused. "No words would ever be adequate enough to show you my gratitude for what you've done for Kinwick these past several years. You have taken great care of us, Raynor. All of us."

He put a hand atop hers and squeezed it. "But Geoffrey is home now. It's time for me to return to Ashcroft."

"I hope you will not be a stranger to us."

"Of course not," he assured her. "But you need time with Geoffrey now, while I must see to things at home."

"Are they so very bad?"

He shrugged. "I hope Gobert has exaggerated the situation, but I have prepared myself for the worst." Raynor looked up and saw that

Geoffrey was walking toward them.

His cousin threw an arm about him. "The twins said you are off soon."

"I am."

"You should at least stay for the noon meal," Merryn chided. "It will be served soon."

"No. I'm ready to be on the road. 'Twill be dark by the time I arrive."

"I'll walk with you to the stables," Geoffrey offered.

"I'll see that your things are brought from your chamber and waiting for you," Merryn promised. She turned and headed toward the keep.

The two men left for the stables. Raynor greeted everyone they passed. He'd become so much a part of life at Kinwick that he knew all by name. Still, he had nothing to show for putting his own life on hold for several years. Like any man, he longed for a wife and children of his own. He wished for love, stability, and purpose.

That, too, would have to wait, at least until he knew what the situation was at Ashcroft.

They reached the stables and Geoffrey ordered a groom to have Fury saddled.

Geoffrey turned to Raynor, tears brimming in his eyes. Since Geoffrey had returned, he wore his emotions close to the surface—something the stoic Geoffrey of old never had revealed.

"I can never repay you for the loving care you bestowed upon Merryn and the twins in my absence. Thank you for your friendship, which goes back as far as my memory does." He gripped Raynor's arm. "Know that you'll always have a home with us."

Raynor threw his arms around Geoffrey and pounded him hard on the back.

"You and your family mean the world to me, Cousin. Thank you for your love and friendship." He spied the groom bringing Fury and released Geoffrey. "I'll visit again soon." Raynor mounted and waved before he spurred his horse on.

Trotting through the inner bailey, he reached the stairs that led up to the keep and found Merryn waiting. She handed him a bag and he tied it to his horse.

"Take care, Raynor. Try to come for Christmas if you can. If not sooner."

"I will do my best."

"Godspeed."

He nodded to Gilbert, the captain of Geoffrey's guard, and to the twins as they jumped up and down, waving wildly at him as he rode by.

Crossing into the outer bailey, he motioned the gatekeeper as he approached. The man signaled for the gates to be opened and Raynor rode through without breaking stride. As he galloped away from Kinwick, he didn't look back.

Raynor wondered if and when he would return.

CHAPTER FOUR

"SHOULD WE STOP soon, Tolly?" Beatrice asked. She hoped the servant would agree to the suggestion since the jostling of the rickety cart had her insides feeling like runny jam. She dreaded the remainder of the trip and wished their destination was closer.

They had left home three days ago. She rode in the back of the cart, as far from the horse as she could get. To steady herself from the bumps in the road, she braced her back against the trunk and protected her lute by keeping it in her lap. The instrument was her most precious possession. Playing it had saved her sanity many times.

They'd camped in the woods on both of the previous nights, making sure to set their fire back from the road to avoid other travelers. With coin scarce, Beatrice looked forward to spending the night at the convent tomorrow night. She was already tired of sleeping on the unforgiving ground. Tolly had explained, for a small donation, travelers were able to enjoy the hospitality of the nuns.

Her servant had lit a lantern in the cart in case it grew dark before they reached a good campsite. She deliberately faced away from the horse, focusing on whatever she could see. She hated that she feared the beasts, but that fear had remained with her ever since her father's death.

"Just a bit farther, my lady. There's a stream where we can water the horse and refresh ourselves."

Beatrice trusted him completely. Tolly had traveled throughout the south of England with his father when he was growing up.

She had high hopes her grandfather's friend would not only take her in but would offer work to her servant, as well. Tolly had proved to be loyal to her grandfather over the years. He had been present when Beatrice arrived with her mother and had remained a part of her life.

There was no guarantee she'd find a home in the north. Especially after she'd acted so boldly, penning a lie to Sir Henry in regard to her upcoming visit to Brookhaven. Lying was a sin and it weighed on her conscience. Mayhap she would be able to confess tomorrow when they reached the convent. That way, she could come to Sir Henry with a clean heart.

Beatrice toyed with several ideas on how to approach the nobleman once they arrived. She might offer to act as a companion to his grandson's bride. When the couple had children, looking after them would be another task in which she could be useful. Since they'd left the manor house, she'd done nothing but think of ways to discuss her situation with Sir Henry.

Beatrice also prayed in earnest to the Holy Mother to give her the right words for when she spoke to the nobleman. If Sir Henry did not grant her refuge, she had no idea what she and Tolly would do once the money she'd sewn into the hem of her *cotehardie* was exhausted.

She thrust her hand into her pocket. Her fingers brushed against her mother's ruby ring. She knew better than to wear it out on the road. Such a fine piece of jewelry would bring unnecessary attention. Still, she liked having it within her grasp because it gave her comfort.

"What's that?" Tolly asked, surprise in his voice.

Beatrice turned to look at the road and saw a dark shape in the middle of their path. With dusk falling, though, she couldn't make out what the obstacle might be.

Tolly slowed the cart and leaned over to pick up the lantern. He stood and held it high.

"It's a man. I must see to him." The servant eased himself down from the driver's seat and reached for the lantern to guide his way.

She climbed down from the cart, as well. If the man was injured or ill, she could help.

They approached the still figure. Beatrice checked his body, finding no apparent wounds. Perhaps a weak heart had caused his collapse.

Tolly handed her the lantern and squatted next to the stranger. He rolled the man from his side to his back.

Without warning, the man shrieked. His right hand swung up. Beatrice caught the glint of steel in the light. Before she could cry out in warning, the man shoved a blade into Tolly's gut and wrenched it up.

She watched in horror as Tolly's eyes widened in surprise. He howled in pain and fell back as his hands grabbed for the buried dagger. As the stranger sat up, Beatrice ran back to the cart, the lantern swinging wildly at her side. Tolly kept an ax in the cart which he used to chop wood. She would threaten this man with it.

But as she set the lantern in the cart and reached for the ax, she found a second man waiting in the bed. He'd already opened her trunk and was rifling through it, tossing clothes and books aside. A book hit the lantern and knocked it over, spilling oil everywhere. The clothes scattered in the bed of the wagon caught fire. The man sprang up and stomped at the flames. Beatrice latched onto the ax and swung it at his feet. He lost his balance and plunged headfirst into the growing fire. An earsplitting scream erupted as he scrambled to his feet, his clothes now in flames.

Suddenly, the thief who'd stabbed Tolly grabbed her from behind. His arms locked around her waist as he lifted her from her feet. Beatrice held fast to the ax. Though she struggled to breathe, she kicked her captor as hard as she could as she watched the other highwayman fall from the flaming cart. He hit the ground and didn't move. Beatrice landed several more blows against the man who held her. He finally released her, cursing loudly.

Stumbling away, she raised her ax protectively as the highwayman advanced in her direction. When he drew close, she swung the weapon at him. He dodged the blade and made for the burning cart, reaching in to rescue her lute from the advancing flames.

"Seems something good's come from this." The robber leered at her as he retreated from the vehicle. "This will fetch a good price—same as you—once I'm done with you."

Instead of his words causing fear, they riled Beatrice into action. Rushing at him, she swung the ax around and brought it forward as hard as she could. It landed where his head joined his neck. He dropped her lute and clutched at the ax embedded deeply in his flesh as he crumpled to the ground.

Beatrice stared in horror at what she had done.

Her gaze skimmed the fire and carnage surrounding her as she tried to comprehend what had occurred. Only minutes ago, they had been driving down the road, ready to make camp for the night. Now, Tolly and two strangers were dead.

She heard a moan come from the burned robber and realized that he still lived. Despite what he had done, she rushed to his side. His charred fingers tightened around her ankle, causing her to panic.

"Nay!" she cried, trying to shake him off as he clutched her. She stomped on his blackened arm and he released her. Running back to the cart, she stumbled against it. Immediately, flames licked at the edge of her cloak and Beatrice screamed. She had no time to unfasten the garment and toss it away. Instead, she dropped to the ground, rolling in the dirt to extinguish the flames.

And then she spied a third stranger crouching next to her beloved lute.

RAYNOR'S SPIRITS SANK as he drew closer to Ashcroft. He loved his ancestral home, but sadness lingered ever since Peter's wife died in childbirth several years ago. She had been a delicate creature and had already miscarried twice before carrying their third child to term. The midwife had done what she could, but his brother had watched his wife die. Hours later, his newborn son died in his arms.

Peter Le Roux had never been the same man.

Always quiet and preferring solitude over the company of others, Peter withdrew after he lost his family. Ashcroft was run under the careful supervision of Gobert, their efficient and caring steward, since Peter neglected most of his duties.

Raynor wished his mother were still alive. She had been a strong-willed woman—much like Merryn de Montfort—and she would never have tolerated her older son's failures. But she had died of a fever four springs ago, mere months after Peter's wife and child had gone to their graves.

His brother swore never to remarry, claiming he would wait to be reunited with his wife in the next life. That meant Ashcroft and the title would one day fall to Raynor if he outlived his brother.

He thought back to the message Gobert had sent to him at Kinwick. The steward begged Raynor to return home. He revealed the estate was falling into disrepair and that Peter had no interest in fixing the issues. If change did not occur soon, Raynor would have no inheritance to claim.

It was time to do whatever it took to bring his brother from the depths of his despair. Raynor berated himself for spending so much time with Merryn and the troubles she had encountered when he should have devoted more of his efforts toward Peter and Ashcroft. Raynor knew that somehow, some way, he would get through to his brother. They owed it to their tenants and the memory of their late parents.

Twilight turned into dusk, so he slowed Fury's pace. Though familiar with the road, he did not want the horse to stumble and break a leg when it was only a short ride to Ashcroft.

Wait.

Off in the distance, he heard something odd. Raynor pulled up on the reins and listened. An unearthly scream echoed in the night air. He urged his horse on, his heart racing. The screams were lost in the pounding of the hooves along the road. Raynor spotted a bright light ahead of him. As he rode closer, he realized it came from a fire. Fury flew the rest of the way, and Raynor tried to take in the scene before him.

A woman rolled about in the dirt and then stopped. There was a body on the ground next to a burning cart. A man with an ax buried in his neck lay motionless a few yards away. Another body was several feet in front of the cart.

By the Christ, what had happened here?

Raynor dismounted and approached the woman, not wanting to alarm her. She struggled to her hands and knees and staggered toward the burning cart. He could see by the light of the fire that part of her cloak had burned away. He didn't know if she had been injured, but he must stop her before she reached the vehicle, which looked on the verge of collapse.

A man huddled near the cart tried rising to his feet. Raynor had missed this stranger in all the mayhem. The woman roared in anger and threw herself at the man, landing on his back. Her arms fastened around his neck as she locked her legs about his waist.

"Drop my lute!" she demanded.

With one hand, the man tried to pry her fingers apart while his other hand held fast to a lute. Raynor realized this man and some of the scattered dead were highwaymen who'd attacked the woman, looking for things to steal.

The thief began turning in circles as he grappled with the woman. Raynor raced toward the pair, motioning for the woman to let go of the man. She shook her head and continued to hang on.

The robber flung the lute aside and Raynor caught it in mid-air. Gently, he placed it on the ground. Seeing her lute was safe, the woman released her hold on the thief and sprang away.

Her sudden move threw the highwayman off-balance. Though he faltered, he still whipped a dagger from his belt and wheeled around to attack her. Then the man froze, catching sight of Raynor beside him.

Raynor's anger exploded. He unsheathed his sword and brandished it before running it through the man.

CHAPTER FIVE

Beatrice tried to catch her breath, only to have it taken away again as she watched the handsome newcomer put a quick end to her attacker. The robber fell to the ground. The man who towered over him with a grim expression on his face pulled his sword from the body, wiped the blood off on the dead man's clothing and then sheathed it.

He shot a look her way and started to speak, but the cry of the frantic horse attached to the cart distracted him. She watched as the cart started to split apart as the horse tried to break free. She was afraid the animal would trample Tolly's body. The kind stranger reached the horse the moment the cart collapsed. He snatched the tangled reins and tried to calm the frightened beast. Beatrice shivered as the horse snorted and stomped its feet. She retreated several steps, her fear of horses ever present.

The man led the horse from the smoldering remains of the vehicle. He stroked the animal's neck and spoke to it softly. Beatrice turned back to her grandfather's trusted servant and a lump formed in her throat. Wordlessly, Beatrice made her way to the body and knelt beside him. Tears blurred her vision as she stroked his cold cheek.

Profound sadness overtook her at Tolly's senseless death. If she had felt alone before, now she truly was. Everyone from her past had been taken away.

"My lady?"

Beatrice glanced over her shoulder and found the stranger standing behind her. He offered his hand and she took it.

Though she hadn't met many men in her isolated life, she knew, beyond a doubt, this tall, broad knight was the handsomest man she'd ever meet.

Though she should fear being alone with a stranger in the middle of nowhere, instinct told Beatrice this was a good man who would treat her with respect.

"My lady," he repeated. "Could you tell me what happened here?"

She brushed the tears from her cheeks with the back of her hands and nodded. Taking a moment to compose herself, she was glad that this knight did not rush her.

In that brief moment, Beatrice decided to lie to protect herself.

"I was traveling with my dear servant to my wedding at Brookhaven."

"I see."

For now, she would do nothing to dispel the man of this notion—at least until she knew more about him.

"We've been journeying for three days to Sir Henry Stollers' estate, which is far to the north. We were about to stop for the night and make camp at a nearby stream."

"I am familiar with it," the knight said.

"Just as twilight fell, we came upon something blocking the road. Tolly stopped our cart, and we both climbed down. As we approached the form, we discovered that it was a man. We didn't know how he came to be there, whether he had collapsed or been trampled by a horse or if he had fallen ill."

She dug her nails into the palms of her hands, fighting through the memories of the recent violence. She took a calming breath and pressed on.

"The man stabbed poor Tolly with a knife, so I ran for the ax in the cart."

The knight frowned. "And what did you plan to do with this ax?"

"Why, frighten the man away!" she exclaimed. "I assumed he was going to rob us. I wanted him gone so that I could tend to Tolly's wound." Beatrice halted as the images kept playing in her mind. "But I found a second man in the cart, going through my trunk. Somehow, the lantern I'd held overturned and started the fire. After that, things became a blur. The robber's clothing caught fire and he fell from the cart. Then the man who had been in the middle of the road grabbed me. I struggled free, but he tried to take my lute. I had the ax and . . ." She searched for words, not finding any to describe what had happened. "Well, then my cloak caught fire. I managed to put out the fire."

She glanced down at what remained of the tattered cloak. "Then another thief appeared. He took my lute before the flames reached it."

"This lute must mean a great deal to you."

"Aye. It has comforted me in good times and bad, my lord. I would do anything to keep it safe."

"I saw exactly what lengths you were willing to go to in order to retrieve it from the robber."

A flush crept up her neck. "I will admit that I was determined. I have a great fondness for my lute."

"Indeed." He paused. "I am sorry that you lost your servant."

She bit her trembling lip, unable to speak. She couldn't imagine life without the quiet, steady servant. Only now, she realized how much she'd relied on Tolly.

The knight interrupted her thoughts. "Did others travel with you?"

"Nay," she said. "Both my mother and grandfather passed away a sennight ago. We were . . . close. They were my whole world."

"And your father?" he asked gently.

She shook her head. "He died long ago when I was but five."

Determination filled his face. "I want you to know that you may trust me implicitly, my lady, despite all that has happened to you in these woods. I am Sir Raynor Le Roux, a knight of the realm. I was traveling from Lord Geoffrey de Montfort's estate of Kinwick to my family's home of Ashcroft, where my brother is baron, when I came upon you and your misfortunes. 'Tis my duty as a knight to see to your safety and well-being."

"And I am Lady Beatrice Bordel." She smiled. "Hopefully, you feel you can trust me, despite the fact that when you came upon me, I appeared as a wild woman might."

"You only defended what was yours." He gestured over his shoulder. "Ashcroft is a short ride from here. I would ask that you return there with me so that I can see to your immediate needs."

She glanced at the destroyed cart and realized that every item she owned—beyond her lute—had gone up in flames. Nothing else remained. She had no home and only the clothes on her back. Tears began to well in her eyes as she took in the enormity of her situation.

Beatrice picked up her lute, glad her beloved instrument had been saved from the fire. Suddenly, she seemed colder than she'd ever been. Her entire body quaked. Her knees buckled and she slipped to the ground.

Then she found herself standing once more. Raynor Le Roux's arms came about her. He enveloped her in an immense yet comforting heat. Beatrice buried her face in his chest.

RAYNOR TENDERLY HELD BEATRICE BORDEL as she cried. He couldn't blame her. Not only had she recently lost two people close to her heart, she'd also witnessed the death of her devoted servant and her own life being threatened by thieves. That forced the lady to take violent action. The man on the ground didn't put that ax in his own neck. Lady Beatrice had done so—and she would have to live with her actions for the rest of her life. Raynor could only imagine what might have happened to the noblewoman if he hadn't come along when he did.

He looked at what little remained of the burned cart and the shell of her trunk, realizing that she probably had all her worldly possessions with her. Nothing had survived the fire. A few stray pieces of parchment fluttered in the wind, all that was left of what he guessed to be treasured books that accompanied her to a new life.

The only thing this poor woman could lay claim to was her lute.

Pity filled him. No one should have to face such circumstances, much less alone.

As he held her, he hoped to ease her fears. He rubbed his large hands up and down her back, providing warmth and comfort.

Her sobs stopped. As he repositioned her in his protective embrace, that's when he became aware of her physical presence as a woman. Soft in all the right places. A foot shorter than he, his chin rested atop her silky, dark hair. Everything about having her in his arms felt right.

But she was betrothed to Sir Henry.

Raynor eased away from her. He placed his hands on her shoulders and put some distance between them while still holding her steady.

"I will escort you to my home. Though you have lost your possessions, there are ample clothes at Ashcroft. My sisters wed many years ago. I lost my mother a few years back, and we can also draw from her chest to make sure you have a variety of things to wear."

He paused, watching her take in his words. "I will accompany you to your betrothed's estate, my lady. I know my brother will allow a guard to come with us. You are perfectly safe in my care until I hand you over to Sir Henry."

She worried her lip, mulling what he'd told her. Raynor didn't rush her decision.

"I suppose that would be the wisest course of action," she finally agreed. "And it's not Sir Henry Stollers I marry. Sir Henry was my grandfather's friend when they fostered together years ago. Sir Henry has a grandson named Edwin."

"Have you met Edwin Stollers?" Raynor found himself jealous of a man he'd never seen. The nobleman would gain quite a bride in this courageous young woman. Raynor had never met anyone he'd admired more. Lady Beatrice's bravery this night in an impossible situation, coupled with her iron will to survive, put to shame most men. Her indomitable spirit had certainly earned his lasting respect.

"No," she said thoughtfully. "But Grandfather thought the world of Sir Henry. He truly looked forward to our journey to Brookhaven and renewing their friendship. In his letters to my grandfather, Sir

Henry described his grandson as a fine man. I have no reason to doubt him."

"When is your wedding?"

She jumped, looking startled at his question. "Ah . . . the wedding is . . . in about three months' time. No specific date has been set. Grandfather and I were simply to journey to Brookhaven when . . ." Her voice trailed off and Raynor knew she must be thinking of her grandfather's death.

"Then we have plenty of time to go to Ashcroft first," he declared. "I have not been home in several months. I must fulfill a few duties there, but then I'll be happy to escort you north for your wedding. We can even send a messenger to Sir Henry to notify him that you will be delayed."

Lady Beatrice started to speak, but it looked as if she changed her mind. He wouldn't worry about the details now. The important thing was to get her safely to Ashcroft.

Raynor released her and then motioned to the horse that he'd rescued from the cart and loosely tied to a tree. "If you ride, you might want to sit atop a horse that you are familiar with. And if you don't, then you may ride with me."

"I won't ride upon any beast! I shall walk to this . . . Ashcroft."

Her angry outburst puzzled Raynor. "But it would be an hour or longer to do so, Lady Beatrice. By riding—"

"I said I will *not* ride."

Pushing aside his frustration at her odd reaction, he tried again to convince her. "Surely, you can make an exception in such circumstances, my lady. It's grown dark. I must see you protected behind Ashcroft's walls."

"Do you not have ears to hear with, Raynor Le Roux? I said that I will walk."

For a minute, Beatrice Bordel looked like Alys de Montfort, a child who intended to have her way. Then he looked deeper and believed he saw fear in her eyes.

"What troubles you, my lady? You showed tremendous courage

this evening. You wielded an ax against highwaymen, ready to defend yourself and your servant. You physically attacked a man twice your size. Yet you will not sit a horse and ease our way?"

Raynor watched fear engulf her as her breathing became ragged and her body began to quake again.

"Nay! I cannot!" she cried, wrapping her arms tightly about her, as if to ward off some unknown threat.

He stood there a moment, uncertain what to do. Part of him thought he should simply place her on Fury and be done with it, but it disturbed him to think that any trust he'd built with her might be shattered by such a thoughtless action.

Mayhap a different approach would work. "Why are you so afraid of horses, Lady Beatrice?"

Raynor watched her begin to collapse and reached out to catch her. He drew her close. Once again, he enjoyed the way she fit next to him.

She did not speak for some minutes. He left her to her thoughts, deciding she would tell him what he needed to know in good time. Finally, he released her.

Beatrice raised her eyes to his. "I have not been atop a horse since the day I turned five," she whispered. "The day my father died."

CHAPTER SIX

BEATRICE COULDN'T BELIEVE SHE had confessed her greatest weakness to this man. No one knew how she felt about horses. Her invalid mother had not cared about anything beyond her sickroom, so Beatrice never confided in her. She suspected her grandfather had an inkling about it, but being a man of action and few words, he never pushed her to discuss her feelings. Tolly had cared for their lone horse—grooming and feeding it—while she'd taken care of the chickens and goat. She gave the horse a wide berth anytime she tended to the other animals. She rarely left the manor house, but on the few occasions she did, Beatrice rode in the back of the cart as she had on their journey north.

She glanced at the knight's giant steed and shuddered at the thought of going near the beast, much less sitting atop it.

Turning back to the nobleman, Beatrice saw the concern etched upon his brow. It struck her that this handsome man really cared about her well-being. Raynor Le Roux was sincere in his intent to see her to safety.

"My father was a knight, as you are, my lord. My earliest memories are of him taking me from my mother's arms and lifting me to sit next to him in the saddle. We would ride Blaze through the meadow while Mother cheered us on. I recall how I would cry out for him to go faster and faster. The world rushed by so fast, it became a blur."

Beatrice paused, willing herself to keep calm. "I don't remember exactly what happened that day, but Blaze faltered as we galloped through an empty field. Both Father and I were thrown from the saddle. I thought Blaze would trample us. I hit the ground so hard that I couldn't breathe." She crossed her arms protectively in front of her.

"Father... he... did not survive the fall. He broke his neck." She pushed aside the image ingrained in her memory.

"And you haven't gone near a horse in all these years?" the knight asked quietly.

"Nay." The word came out a whisper.

Raynor nodded in understanding. "I can assure you that Fury is an extremely good horse."

Her eyes flew to the beast, then back to its master. Beatrice shook her head. "I am sorry, my lord. Simply hearing the animal's name frightens me."

He looked fondly at his horse. "Despite his fierce name, Fury is as gentle as a lamb. I promise you I will keep him at an easy pace. You would be perfectly safe in my arms."

A part of Beatrice longed to be in those very arms again. She'd never felt more protected than when this man had held her close. Though she had no experience with men, this gallant knight had rescued her from a fate worse than death. She could tell he was a man marked by honor and took his knightly oath seriously.

How she wished her life had been different and that her father had lived. Beatrice knew he would have showered her with affection and attention. Her father also would have found a just nobleman to be her wedded husband and ensure her future was secure. But none of that had come to pass, and she was alone in the world. Why couldn't she find a good man such as Raynor Le Roux, one she could share her life with, laugh with, and love long and well? She would give anything to be the wife of a knight as noble as Sir Raynor.

But his reverent tone when he spoke of Ashcroft led her to believe that the place must be a huge estate. Besides, the man was well over a score—so surely he had a wife and children waiting for him at home. Even if he didn't, Beatrice had led him to believe she was promised to Edwin Stollers. Though she had never directly referred to him as her betrothed, she *had* mentioned her wedding. Because of that, this chivalrous knight would never foster any personal feelings for her. Beatrice determined to put aside such wishes and dreams, for they could never occur.

"Thank you, Sir Raynor, but I can't. Call it childish fear, but nothing could ever entice me to ride on a horse." She bowed her head. "I'm sorry, my lord."

"I understand, my lady."

Beatrice gazed into his eyes and believed he truly did.

The conversation over, Raynor lifted Tolly's body and placed him face down on their horse. After carefully securing the body, he led the horse to Fury and fastened the animal behind his.

"Let us set out, my lady. We have a good way to walk and no time to waste."

She reclaimed her lute and faced him. "Just because I choose to walk doesn't mean you have to do the same. You may ride, my lord."

"And leave a lady on the ground to trail after me?" He shook his head. "Heaven forbid that I would be so callous. 'Twould go against all I stand for."

"Then I'll follow you and the horses."

Raynor approached Fury and stroked the horse fondly, murmuring words too low for her to catch. Then he pulled an apple from his pocket and placed it in his palm. The horse eagerly took the offered treat.

He took the reins. "Do not fall too far behind me, Lady Beatrice," he warned. "It grows dark. I would have you close by." He pulled on the reins and both horses started after him as he led the way, leaving the dead highwaymen behind without a backward glance.

Beatrice fell into step. She knew he wasn't pleased at the distance she put between her and the animals because he kept turning around to check where she was.

"You must come closer, my lady," he finally called out.

She did as he asked, catching up with him. "You can walk beside me," he said patiently. "Away from the horses. The reins are long enough that we can be in front of Fury and not cause you any discomfort."

They walked for several minutes, taking care where they trod, but the toe of her shoe hit a rock. Her foot slipped out from underneath her.

Raynor dropped the reins and grabbed her by her elbows before she fell.

She could have stared at his beautiful face forever as he steadied her.

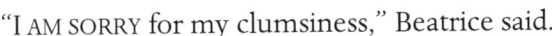

"I AM SORRY for my clumsiness," Beatrice said.

"You have nothing to apologize for, my lady," Raynor assured her. "It's grown quite dark. Anyone—man or woman—could have stumbled easily. Why don't you take hold of me in order to steady yourself?" He offered her the crook of his arm so she could slide her hand through it.

"Thank you, my lord." Beatrice shifted her lute to her left arm and then took his hand.

Never had Raynor experienced such a jolt of excitement from a woman's touch. He glanced down at their joined hands and thought how right it seemed. It surprised him. At the moment, Lady Beatrice was filthy and disheveled, her clothing singed and reeking from the smoke of the fire. Yet, his pulse quickened and his skin prickled as if the time to ride into battle neared.

He pushed aside the odd feeling and bent to retrieve Fury's reins. "Come, my lady." Raynor squeezed her hand gently. "We'll arrive at Ashcroft in no time."

They began walking hand-in-hand. Deliberately ignoring the feelings that churned within him, he decided to tell her something about where they journeyed.

Anything to occupy his mind.

"Ashcroft is my brother's estate. It has a small keep when compared to most, with only forty families farming the land and tending to the livestock. Peter became the baron upon my father's death, which happened just after my twin sisters wed, about eight years ago."

"You have a brother and twin sisters?" she marveled. "Oh, I always wished for siblings. Growing up without any was a true hardship."

Raynor laughed. "I was close to my brother since we are only a year apart. But my sisters? They were four years younger, always playing with dolls and talking about clothes. I love them dearly, as any brother would, but both are pretty girls with empty heads."

"My lord!" Beatrice chastised and he heard the indignation in her voice. "I feel I must stand up for these women. Surely, they must have more substance than you claim. Especially now," she mused, "for they would be grown women, married and with children, I suppose."

"They are indeed. Both have two children each. I hate to disappoint you, my lady, but they remain women who talk about nothing but... womanly things."

She chuckled. "And what would you have them speak of?"

He shrugged. "I'm not sure." He thought a moment. "What do you like to discuss? Or do?"

She gave him a warm smile. "I enjoy my music." She nodded at her lute. "I sing and play most every day. I even compose my own songs."

"Now that is far more interesting than talk of the colors to dye a *cotehardie* or what caul should be worn during the Easter season. Do you write lyrics about clothes or womanly chores?" he teased.

This time she laughed aloud. "Nay. I write of the stories my grandfather told me. He could read in English and Latin. In fact, my name comes from Latin. Beatrice means *she who brings happiness*. My songs are about the exploits of Odysseus and Beowulf. Or sometimes I sing of things in nature, such as a lark's song or a summer storm."

"I look forward to hearing you sing and play. Mayhap you would grace us with your songs during your brief stay at Ashcroft."

"I would be happy to do so, my lord. I can even sing for you now if you wish. It has always brought me comfort. I know it would help me forget my sorrow."

Beatrice began to hum softly, a sweet melody that echoed the wistful longing within him. As they continued down the road, she began to put words to her song. Raynor became entranced with her voice. It could fall low, as a hushed whisper, before it soared to clear heights.

She continued to entertain him until they reached Ashcroft lands. He wished that they arrived in daylight so she could see the estate better. He was happy that she seemed to have forgotten about the horses that traipsed after them. Raynor determined that he would help her conquer her fear of them before they set out for Brookhaven. It was the least he could do to help her as she moved on to her new life in the north.

"Oh!" she exclaimed. "I thought you said Ashcroft was a small place."

Raynor studied the high gate as they approached. Neither it nor the keep seemed large to him. He and Geoffrey had fostered at Sir Lovel's vast estate, spending their formative years there, and it was the largest he'd known. Kinwick, Geoffrey's home, also was a huge property. Raynor supposed he judged Ashcroft against those places, but he had a fondness for Ashcroft because it was home.

They approached the gate and he shouted up, "Gatekeeper. 'Tis I, Raynor Le Roux. Open at once!"

No one answered him. The gate remained fastened. The tiny hairs on the back of his neck stood on end.

"Gatekeeper! Are you there?" he called again. "Open up, I say!"

He heard a faint scraping and then saw a face peering down at them, though he could not make out who sat guard.

"Are things well at Ashcroft?" he demanded. "Let me in so that I may see for myself."

"Give me a minute, my lord," a voice told him. Raynor believed the man had been asleep at his station. If so, a strong punishment would be in store for this lapse in duty.

They waited in silence some minutes. His concern grew as he noticed no one patrolled the wall-walk above. Finally, the gate drew wide. The same man—no, a boy—had opened the gates, leaving his post above to do so.

Raynor released Beatrice's hand and marched toward the lad. "Why has a mere child been left to mind the gate? And where are the men that should have opened it to me, much less those who should patrol the wall-walk at night?"

"I am Neal, my lord. You have been gone many months. Ashcroft has changed in that time."

"How so?"

The boy shrugged. "You will have to talk to the steward about this." His lip curled. "Or your brother. Not that we see hide nor hair of him these days."

Raynor's gut clenched. He thought Gobert's missive had exaggerated. Now he wasn't so sure.

"Close and lock the gates and get back to your post," he ordered. "And Neal?" He waited till the boy looked him in the eye. "I'm sure I would never catch you sleeping while on duty." His tone made it clear what would happen if he did.

The boy dropped his head, as guilty as a small child who had been caught stealing sweets. "Aye, my lord."

Raynor waited till the gates were secured and Neal had scurried off.

He turned to Beatrice, who wore a guarded expression. "We'll walk the horses to the stables. They need to be rubbed down and fed."

She nodded, and Raynor took her hand. "It's dark still and you are unfamiliar with Ashcroft," he gave as an excuse to touch her again. As before, her hand in his seemed the most natural thing in the world.

No one stirred as they cut through the outer and inner baileys. It did not surprise him since the hour grew late. They arrived at the stable and found another boy sleeping just inside the doors. Raynor woke him.

"Where is Old Sam, our head groom?" he asked.

"Gone," the boy informed him.

"Gone where?"

"He be dead and gone."

Raynor was sorry to hear the news. Old Sam had passed along much of his knowledge regarding horses to Raynor. In turn, Raynor had done the same when he fostered with Sir Lovel, helping Michael Devereux, a chubby lad who feared horses. Raynor had spent hours with the frightened page, teaching him to understand the creatures and be a proficient rider. Old Sam would have been proud that his advice had helped Devereux to conquer his fears. The lessons regarding horses had changed the boy's life. Raynor was happy to have been a part of Michael Devereux's maturing and idly wondered where the young knight might be now.

He turned his thoughts back to the present. "Who minds the stables now?"

"My father and I. Old Sam was my grandfather."

"Ah, you are Brice then."

The boy frowned. "You know me?"

"I know everyone at Ashcroft," Raynor assured him. "Or at least those who remain."

Brice nodded eagerly. "Lots of soldiers left. Everyone talks how Master has let things fall into . . ." His voice trailed off as the boy realized who he was speaking to.

"We'll have a good talk tomorrow, Brice. For now, my horse, Fury, and the other need looking after. Are you up to the task?"

"I suppose." Brice looked unsure at this request.

Raynor realized the child hadn't the height to remove the saddle, much less reach high enough to curry the horses properly.

"What if I help you this time? Caring for horses may be one of my favorite tasks in the world," he told the lad.

"Thank you!"

He looked to Beatrice. "My lady, would you care to wait here? We shall be a few minutes, then I will escort you into the keep."

"Yes, my lord." She stepped back a few paces, and he led the horses to two empty stalls opposite one another.

Raynor loosened the restraints holding Tolly's body to the horse and moved the dead servant to another vacant stall. He would need to discuss the man's burial with their priest. He then instructed Brice in the basics, which the boy seemed to know from either Old Sam or his own father. Raynor promised to return tomorrow and work with Brice more closely.

"I have high expectations when it comes to my horse. Fury deserves the best of care."

Brice promised to watch Fury carefully until Raynor came to the stables to give the lad another lesson. Raynor lifted his bundle of possessions that he'd placed in the corner and headed for the entrance.

Beatrice waited in the same place he'd left her. Wordlessly, he captured her hand in his and led her toward the keep. They entered and paused in the great hall. Raynor looked across it, surprised to see that only about half of those who normally bedded down there were present.

"Sir Raynor," a voice called softly behind him.

He turned to find Gobert approaching. The steward looked half a score older since Raynor had last seen him. He released Beatrice's hand and strode toward him.

"Thank the Christ you have returned, my lord," Gobert said in a rush. "I have done my best trying to keep Ashcroft from falling into ruin." He hesitated. "And I am afraid your brother might very well have gone mad."

CHAPTER SEVEN

BEATRICE STOOD IN the shadows, alarmed by the man's words.

What on earth had she gotten into?

She had attached herself to a complete stranger and come to his home without question, dazzled by his good looks and gallant ways. But what little she'd seen since their arrival concerned her. Though unfamiliar with how life in a castle unfolded, this place seemed be run shoddily. No one defended it. Only young boys were about. The stench of old rushes, rotting food, and piss coming from the great hall assaulted her nose.

And now Raynor Le Roux had just been told that his own brother might be mad?

Beatrice shuddered. Ashcroft was nothing like what Sir Raynor had told her. Yet, in the knight's defense, he also seemed surprised by what they had come across since their arrival.

"Mad?" Raynor hissed. "What are you talking about, Gobert? You said nothing of this in your message to me."

The rotund, balding man looked apologetic. "I'm sorry to keep it from you, my lord. But you have been gone for some time—and when you have returned these past few years, you've only stayed for brief periods."

Raynor glared down at the man. "So, you're saying that I haven't paid enough attention to circumstances on my quick sojourns home? You believe that I have been remiss in my duties?"

"Nay, my lord." The man took a step back. "It's not your place to see to the running of Ashcroft. It is Lord Peter's responsibility." He swallowed. "Though I do fear for what goes through his mind these days."

Raynor's balled his hands into fists. "Why do you think he has gone mad, Gobert?"

Beatrice saw how the knight controlled his temper and hoped he could keep it reined in. Being a man of formidable size and strength, she didn't want to see this servant take the brunt of his wrath.

"Rarely anyone sees him, my lord. Lord Peter takes all his meals alone in the solar. Most of his days are consumed by kneeling in prayer, whether in his oratory or the chapel. He goes for weeks without speaking." Gobert paused, looking uncomfortable. "And sometimes Lord Peter . . . he . . . takes off."

"Where? Where does he go?" Raynor demanded.

Gobert shrugged. "We haven't a clue, my lord. He'll simply be gone come morning. No one sees him leave the castle grounds. Occasionally, he's spotted when he emerges from the woods upon his return. I don't know if he lives and sleeps there or what he does. We all fear for his safety when he's gone. And with no one to tell the people what to do while he's away?" He raised his palms and shook his head sadly. "Ashcroft suffers from the lack of strong leadership. That's why I asked you to come home. You're his flesh and blood, my lord, the one he would listen to above all others. Mayhap you can talk some sense into him."

Raynor's mouth set in grim determination. "If I can't, I'll see that the people of Ashcroft receive the proper guidance, Gobert. As Peter's brother, I should have done more. Much more. I let the needs of others distract me. I assure you this will not happen in the future."

Beatrice stepped forward. "I can help you with this endeavor, my lord."

Gobert's eyes widened as he caught sight of her. "Who—"

"This is Lady Beatrice Bordel, Gobert. My lady, this is Gobert, Ashcroft's steward—and my friend," Raynor added quietly. He looked back at the steward. "Lady Beatrice had a run-in with some highwaymen. I've brought her to Ashcroft and guaranteed her safety. As soon as I have set things right here, I plan to escort her north to join her betrothed's family."

"Very good, my lord. Where . . . where would you have her stay?"

"I think we can put her in my sisters' former bedchamber. Does it still contain some of their old clothing?"

Gobert thought a moment. "It should. But the room will be quite musty. It hasn't been aired out since—"

"That's how I can assist you, my lord," Beatrice interrupted. "You asked me earlier what I did with my time. Besides my music, I was in charge of our manor house. I can cook, sew, and clean. I'm afraid you don't have any idea how to set things straight inside the keep, but I'm familiar with such woman's work."

She took another step forward and placed a hand upon his forearm. "Please, let me be useful and help you so that you can concentrate on other matters. I'm not expected at Brookhaven for three months. I can help you right everything here. It's a small way to repay you for the aid you've given me."

Beatrice watched him mull her offer over and saw when he decided to accept it.

"Very well, my lady. It would be nice to have a woman's touch handling affairs inside the keep." He placed his hand atop hers and guided it to the crook of his arm. "I will escort you to the chamber where my sisters slept growing up. It can be the first place you start tomorrow. You should make yourself comfortable there before seeing to other things."

Raynor turned to Gobert. "We'll speak in the morning after we break our fast. Mayhap we can encourage Peter to sit with us while we discuss the running of the estate."

Gobert grimaced. "I'm afraid he's gone again, my lord. Vanished sometime yesterday, and he did not return today."

Beneath her fingers, Beatrice felt Raynor's muscles tighten at this news. "I'll deal with everything, Gobert. I promise. I bid you a good night."

He turned away from the servant and guided her up a large stone staircase. A single sconce cast an inkling of light at the top of the stairs.

"More should be lit," he muttered as they walked down the hallway.

"I'll take an inventory, my lord. I can check to see what's available and what's needed. I'll take stock of how many candles there are and if more should be made. I'll investigate what the larder holds and what herbs are stored and replenish what they lack."

Raynor paused as they came to a doorway. "Your help will be immeasurable, my lady." He frowned. "I regret that I have brought you into such circumstances. I am ashamed of how neglected Ashcroft is and the part I played in it sinking to such a low level."

"But you are not the baron," she reminded him. "It wouldn't have been your place to instruct an older, titled brother on how to run his estate."

A weariness settled over him, thick as a woolen blanket. "Nay. I should have been here. Peter lost his wife and son during childbirth and has mourned for them ever since. Our mother passed soon after that. I should have known what those blows meant to him. 'Twas my place to support him."

"He might not have let you," she said gently. "But you are here now, willing to help Lord Peter in whatever tasks must be accomplished. I'm sure he'll be most grateful for your help."

"We'll see." Raynor sighed. "I wish you good night, Lady Beatrice. Please make use of any clothing you find within. And I hope you won't regret being brought to stay at Ashcroft for a time."

Before she could reassure him, Raynor bent and pressed a chaste kiss upon her brow. Beatrice stilled and gave him a trembling smile.

"Thank you once more for rescuing me, my lord. I am thankful that you came along when you did. I will see you in the morning. Have you a chapel?"

"Aye. If you will allow me, I'll stop by your chamber and escort you to mass and breaking your fast. Good night, my lady," he said softly before he continued down the darkened corridor.

She opened the door and hurried in, closing it behind her. Beatrice leaned against it for support. In all of the disappointments that she had discovered since they'd entered Ashcroft, one good bit of news lingered in her mind.

Raynor Le Roux obviously had no wife or child.

RAYNOR TOSSED AND TURNED. Sleep escaped him as his mind whirled in a thousand directions. No matter how many times he tried to let his mind become a blank, he remained agitated. Guilt weighed heavily upon him. He berated himself for being so enthralled with Merryn and her twins that he had put his own life on hold and been neglectful of his own family for some time.

In truth, he didn't know much about his brother anymore since he'd spent long stretches of time at Kinwick. Even growing up, they were very unlike one another. Where Raynor liked to hunt and fish with friends, his brother pursued solitary interests. Raynor had enjoyed everything about fostering with Sir Lovel, from learning the duties required of a page and squire to the training he undertook to become a knight. He loved the camaraderie with his fellow soldiers, the long hours spent in the yard, and the conversation once training had ended for the day. He enjoyed being in the company of others, always ready to tell a joke or bed a willing wench.

But those carefree days must be put behind him. He must rouse his brother from whatever malaise pulled at him and bring swift changes to Ashcroft. If Peter stayed true to his decision not to marry again—and from Gobert's description, that seemed a distinct possibility—then the estate would eventually come to Raynor. He didn't want the people to suffer in the meantime. Ashcroft must become and remain productive. Whatever it took to guarantee the estate succeeded, even if it meant overstepping his bounds, he would begin in the morning.

Pushing himself to a sitting position, Raynor braced his back against the wall in his chamber. It wasn't only Ashcroft's disrepair that kept him awake tonight.

Beatrice Bordel's image also kept him wide-eyed.

He couldn't believe a mere slip of a woman had him tangled in knots. Raynor still hadn't gotten a clear look at her. He longed to see her in daylight and find out the true color of her eyes and what shade her hair became when sunlight fell upon it. He wanted to run his hands through it, down her back, and more. Much more. He pictured them in an embrace, arms wrapped about one another, as he took his fill of her sweetness.

"God's wounds!" he cried out. He got out of bed and pushed his hands through his thick hair. Would he always be cursed to fall in love with women who were unavailable to him?

Pacing the small chamber, he fought to gain control of the wild ideas that flitted through his head. No woman had ever caused him to behave in such a manner. He must rid himself of these fantasies since Lady Beatrice was promised to another man. His knightly code demanded that he keep his pledge to protect her and deliver her to her betrothed. Nothing untoward could occur between them.

It troubled him that they would live in close contact for several weeks, but he planned to keep his promise to Gobert and bring Ashcroft back to better days. And somehow, he must reach Peter. They had been close once, years ago, despite their different dispositions.

He prayed that his brother remained sane and merely chose to live in seclusion because of his lasting grief. Raynor hoped he held the key that would unlock whatever prison Peter had willingly thrust himself into.

Returning to his bed, he stretched out, placing both hands behind his head and letting his thoughts wander again until he heard footsteps. He sat up.

Who could be lurking about the keep in the dead of night?

Raynor retrieved the sword lying next to his bed and crept to the doorway. Easing the weapon from its sheath, he silently turned the knob.

As he opened the door, a shuffling noise sounded down the corridor to his right. Raynor left his chamber to investigate. He spied a shadowy figure a few doors down and began to stalk it. By the height, it had to be a man.

Closing in, he watched the man pause at the end of the hall in front of the door leading into the solar. Slowly, the shadow turned and faced him.

"Hello, Brother," Peter said.

CHAPTER EIGHT

RAYNOR FROZE AT the familiar voice. A multitude of feelings swirled through him.

"Come in," Peter instructed as he pushed open the door. He crossed the room and lit a candle before he sat upon a bench.

Raynor reluctantly entered the solar. He couldn't remember the last time he'd been invited inside. Its rooms had been the site of many happy occasions while growing up. His last memory, though, was colored by his brother sitting in the very spot he occupied now—only then, Peter's head had been lowered to the table as he wept upon hearing the news of their mother's death.

Closing the door behind him, Raynor took a seat opposite Peter. He studied his brother for a moment as the candle flickered, casting odd shadows upon his brother's face.

"Where have you been?" Raynor demanded.

Peter gave him a wry smile. "I might ask the same of you."

He flinched at the words.

"You always had such a sense of duty," Peter said, shaking his head. "True to your code of chivalry. Marked by your service to the king and the good of your fellow man."

"It's how Father raised us," he answered, "and how Sir Lovel trained the boys fostering under him. Honor and duty were first and foremost."

Peter laughed softly. "You were always so excited about life, Raynor. Enthusiastic about swordplay. Full of vim and vigor. Ready to take on the world. Well, let me tell you, little brother—the world can be a dark place."

"You have allowed it to become so for you," he retorted.

Peter's brows shot up, then understanding dawned on his face. "Ah, you've been talking to Gobert. Our loyal steward is the one who summoned you home, I suppose. You would never come here of your own free will. You sought out adventure—and then coveted Merryn de Montfort. She's enthralled you for a long time." He paused, his lips twitching in amusement. "Did she finally toss you out? Or better yet, did the king find her a new husband to marry since hers ran away? I'll bet he did, one befitting her station, with a title and abundant property."

His brother had always fought his battles with words and knew how to injure his opponent to the quick. Raynor would not rise to the bait Peter offered.

Calmly, he said, "Geoffrey de Montfort has returned to Kinwick."

Peter's wild laughter went on for some minutes, causing Raynor to question his brother's sanity. Wheezing, Peter finally caught his breath. "So, your best friend came home to claim his pretty wife, and that left you out in the cold. Now here you are, ready to chastise me. Oh, I see it in your eyes, Brother. You've never been one to disguise your feelings."

"As far as Ashcroft goes, I have no need to hide anything." Raynor heard the sharpness in his words and softened his tone. "Gobert told me—"

"Oh, I am sure our steward has informed you of many things. That I rarely speak to anyone and disappear for days on end. That I pray more than I breathe and I no longer care for the estate or the people on it."

Raynor stared into the eyes of a man who had become a stranger to him. "Are his words true?"

Peter slammed a hand down on the wooden table. Through gritted teeth he said, "I have not cared for anything—*anything*—since God saw fit to deprive me of my beloved wife and child. I have cursed Him both day and night since that time."

Peter's fists grabbed onto chunks of his hair and squeezed tightly, as if he might rip the hair from his scalp. A wildness appeared in his eyes, making it seem that he danced upon the precipice of madness.

"I spend hours praying for forgiveness every day, for I am weak, Raynor. Weaker than any man I know. I was never physically strong and I became emotionally numbed by all that befell me. Aye, I let the people do as they please. If they work, they shall live. If they don't?" He shrugged. "Then they can starve. I truly don't care what happens to them. Soldiers who pledged their fealty to Father have now deserted me. They call me a coward and feebleminded. Many have fled and moved on."

Peter paused, contemplating his next words. "None of that matters. Do you hear me? If Ashcroft fell down about my ears, it would mean nothing to me. I simply want to be left alone."

"You will not offer leadership?"

"Nay, Brother. You've been prudent enough to stay out of my affairs till now, but you may intervene if you see fit. It's no longer my concern." Peter released the hold he had on his hair. "Do as you wish, but don't disturb me to tell me of your actions. I will return to my suffering in silence."

Peter stood. "Now I ask you to leave me in peace. Or simply leave. You have always done as you wished, Raynor, and been your own man. You are free to come and go as you please. I wash my hands of you and Ashcroft."

His brother went to the door of his bedchamber and entered, softly shutting the door behind him.

Stunned by what his brother had voiced, Raynor sat at the table for some minutes. Peter had always been a pleasant fellow, both kind and sympathetic. Never a great warrior or horseman, but a nobleman who took his responsibilities seriously and cared for those around him. This bitter, vindictive shell of a man proved to be a stranger.

Raynor shuddered to think of the condition he would find Ashcroft in once daylight broke.

Raynor left his chamber long before the sun rose and decided to start with Father Benedict. The old priest slept little at his advanced age, so Raynor ventured to the Ashcroft chapel and found the priest at prayers. He waited until Father Benedict finished and rose to his feet.

"Father?"

The large man turned and his face lit with a smile. "Raynor. 'Tis good to see you, my son. I hope you will grace us with your presence for a little while, for I have missed our talks."

He got straight to the point. "I have learned that Peter has been remiss in his duties as baron."

The man of God shrugged. "Remiss . . . is a kind word. I would say negligent. The keep is filthy and the harvest has barely been started. Half the soldiers have moved on to other liege lords, leaving Ashcroft vulnerable to attack. And Lord Peter doesn't notice what goes on or has decided he doesn't care enough to remedy matters."

"It's the latter, Father. Peter has given me permission to step in and do whatever I see fit. He seems to have washed his hands of any affairs that deal with Ashcroft."

Tears welled in the old man's blue eyes. "Thank the Christ!" he whispered, closing his eyes, his lips moving silently in prayer. Raynor assumed the old man gave praise to God for providing a remedy to a dark situation.

Father Benedict opened his eyes. "What will you do first, my son?"

"'Twill be what you do first, Father. On my way home from Kinwick yesterday, I came upon a traveling noblewoman. Highwaymen had killed her servant and left her with nothing but the clothes on her back. I placed her under my protection and brought her trusted servant's body here to Ashcroft. I would ask that you offer a burial mass for Tolly today and see that he's placed in the ground."

"Of course. I'll excuse two of the men from mass so that they can dig the grave." He snorted. "Not that I have many to choose from."

"What do you mean?" asked Raynor, puzzled by such an odd remark.

The old man shook his head in sorrow. "Less than half of Ashcroft's people attend morning mass with any regularity."

Anger surged through Raynor. His parents had always expected their servants and serfs to attend mass before they broke their fast. His father believed that starting the day in God's good graces would mean He would be bountiful in return.

"Another thing I will see to, Father. I give you my promise that Ashcroft will no longer succumb to laziness and apostasy. The people need direction and leadership, and I plan to provide it."

The priest took hold of Raynor's forearms, his grip surprisingly strong for a man of his advanced age. "It's good to have you back, Raynor Le Roux. You are the answer to my prayers."

Leaving the chapel, Raynor walked through both baileys before he returned to the keep and noticed many things had been neglected. It shamed him to see what had become of his boyhood home. He would ride through the estate lands today and get an idea of where everything stood beyond the walls of the castle.

Mounting the stairs, he proceeded to the chamber Lady Beatrice had been placed in last night and rapped lightly on the door.

BEATRICE HAD BEEN up for a few hours. She had found a candle in the bedchamber and had gone back down the hall to where the candle flickered in its sconce. Lighting her own candle with that flame, she proceeded back to her chamber.

The large room housed an enormous bed. In her mind, she could see the twin sisters who grew up here, giggling and talking far into the night, happy in one another's company. But the room itself needed a thorough cleaning. Though she had fallen into a deep sleep, exhausted by the long day, she'd awakened early and found herself restless. The bedclothes gave off a horribly musty smell. She didn't know how old they were, but they needed a good washing, followed by drying them in strong sunlight. The tattered bed curtains needed to come down and be replaced. The floor and walls should be thoroughly scrubbed—and scrubbed again for good measure. She wondered if all of the rooms in the keep needed such attention and guessed they did.

While exploring the pair of matching chests left behind, Beatrice found many items she could use. Raynor's sisters had left behind several kirtles and smocks and numerous *cotehardies*. While they might be slightly out of style, that wouldn't bother her. Being brought up in the country, she had no idea of the latest fashions at the court in London. Claiming a few of these clothes would more than replace her missing wardrobe. The variety of colors and cuts would also make her more than presentable when she arrived at Sir Henry's estate.

She discovered a few pairs of shoes under the bed. One of the girls obviously had much larger feet because these shoes fell off her foot when she tried them on. The other Le Roux twin had left two pairs of shoes behind, one of them sturdy brown boots. They fit Beatrice as if they had been made for her. She was most excited about finding the boots. She had never owned anything as fine as the soft leather they were made from and decided to wear them today.

After she chose a yellow kirtle and *cotehardie* and dressed for the day, she searched the rest of the chamber. Nothing else held her interest. She did discover a comb with a few teeth missing, but it swept through her hair easily after she unbraided it. Beatrice re-braided her hair, the single plait falling to her waist, and then sat in the chair to await Raynor's arrival.

When the knock sounded, her stomach flipped in a most peculiar way. She realized she was nervous, a new emotion for her. Beatrice answered the door, eager to see the handsome knight again.

"Good morning, my lady. Are you ready to attend mass?"

"Yes, my lord." She took the arm he offered and thought that he seemed weary.

Raynor led them down the hallway to the wide staircase. "I hope you rested well in my sisters' bedchamber."

"I'll admit I was more than tired and fell asleep quickly," she replied. "But when I awoke, I donned some clothing your sisters left behind. They are a decent fit and will be more so after I take a needle to them."

They quickly descended the stairs. He took her to a door leading outside. Shades of gray still colored the world in this early hour.

"Our chapel is small and located inside the walls of Ashcroft." He frowned. "It's very cool this morning. I should have suggested that you bring a cloak."

"I didn't find one in my chamber, but mayhap I will find cloth to make one for myself."

He nodded. "I'm sure your inventory will apprise you of what's available. I'm most grateful for your help, my lady."

They reached the stone chapel and entered.

He bent next to her ear. His lips almost grazed it as he said, "I have spoken to Father Benedict. He will say a mass for Tolly today and see that he is properly buried."

Goosebumps sprang up all over her body as his warm breath caressed her. Beatrice found it hard to breathe. She merely nodded as he pulled away.

She was not used to attending mass on a daily basis. On holy days, her grandfather had taken them to the church in the nearest village. She supposed all the great castles of England housed their own chapels and had their own priests.

When the service ended, Raynor escorted her back to the keep. Now that the sun had risen, Beatrice couldn't help but assess the man at her side, finally seeing him clearly for the first time since they'd met.

She'd known Raynor Le Roux was tall, but in the light, she could see how well-built he was. Well over six feet, the knight radiated strength and confidence. The sun burnished his hair to a rich russet. His eyes were the color of summer grass, a vivid green set in a face that could have been chiseled from stone. High cheekbones and a strong jaw made him handsome beyond belief. It caused her insides to flutter in a way that left her giddy—and confused.

They stepped into the great hall. Her eyes swept across the space and fell upon a group of rowdy soldiers on one side of the room. Others with children gathered on the opposite side and she assumed these were the castle's servants and the serfs who farmed the land.

Raynor brought her to a dais that sat high enough to be able to see everyone gathered in the room. He seated her and a pretty, plump girl brought them bread and ale.

"Eat up," he encouraged. "I fear you will earn your keep these next few weeks as I try to bring a semblance of order back to Ashcroft."

Sipping the cool ale, Beatrice asked, "Will you search for your brother first?" since she knew Gobert had revealed the baron was missing.

A look of distaste crossed Raynor's face. "Nay. Peter returned home last night. We had a most enlightening conversation. Suffice it to say, he's granted me permission to do all I need to restore Ashcroft to its former state. I'm only sorry you have seen it so neglected."

"You have no need to apologize to me." She gazed around the great hall. "This is the grandest room I've ever seen. The manor house I grew up in was tidy but small. I can't wait to see the rest of the keep and all of the castle grounds." She looked back at him and felt the heat rise on her cheeks at his intent stare.

"Promise me, my lady, that you won't roam about without me or a designated escort. Inside the keep is not a problem. But I need to understand the lay of the land before allowing you to move freely about the grounds."

"I understand." Beatrice finished her meal and continued to study those in the room, catching curious glances cast in their direction.

Raynor rose after he finished eating and addressed the crowd. "Good morning," he called out.

The people returned a mumbled greeting. Beatrice noted a wariness in the eyes of many as they turned their full attention upon him.

"I have been gone from Ashcroft often, but I plan to stay and see to its immediate needs in the next couple of months. My brother, Lord Peter, has agreed that I may make any changes needed in order to improve things." He paused. "The first of these adjustments will be for everyone from the captain of the guard to the youngest serving wench to attend daily mass. The Le Roux family keeps Christ in their hearts and at the center of their work. The same should be true for everyone on the estate."

He looked to the trestle tables that seated the group of soldiers. "I will be in the training yard in half an hour's time. I want to see you at practice so I may judge where we stand regarding our defenses. Sir Ralph, you and I will discuss the guard duty schedule, among other matters."

Beatrice saw a bearded man in his forties scowl at the words and assumed that he was Sir Ralph. She would not want to be in his shoes. If this knight had become derelict in his duties, she knew Raynor would tell him in no uncertain terms.

"The soldiers are dismissed," Raynor said.

The benches scraped the floor as the men stood and made their way out of the great hall.

When the last soldier had left, Raynor continued. "I would like to introduce to you Lady Beatrice Bordel." He offered her his hand and she took it. She stood, trying to calm the butterflies in her stomach as the attention of everyone in the room focused on her.

"Lady Beatrice is visiting at Ashcroft before I escort her to her new home at Brookhaven. She has full authority inside the keep. It is up to her to decide what tasks need to be assigned and completed. I ask that you give her due respect and your cooperation." His nose crinkled. "I hope she'll start here in the great hall."

Raynor's head turned slowly, taking in the room. "I'm embarrassed to find rotted food and dog shit flung everywhere," he told the group. "You dishonor my mother's memory and shame Ashcroft by the way you have let the great hall fall into ruin. This kind of behavior will not be tolerated in the future."

Beatrice sank to her seat and watched the people shift uncomfortably. Many lowered their gazes to the ground in shame.

His voice rang out. "I've discovered that the harvest has barely begun. You know we only have about two months to complete it, along with the tying and winnowing. The milling should follow shortly afterward. Failure to do so could lead to starvation. *Your own children* might suffer if you don't put your best effort into this endeavor."

Raynor looked out over the crowd. "Ashcroft has always been a place of plenty. A place where the people worked together for the good of all. Every man, woman, and child took pride in the contributions they made. I expect nothing less from this day forth. We will work together in a spirit of cooperation. I will personally discipline anyone who shirks his duties. Punishment will be swift. Is that understood by all?"

A low murmur was the response. Beatrice observed many glances as workers looked sheepishly at one another.

"I wish for us to, once again, become as a family, bound by our duty, respect, and love for one another, as we were in the past. I'll provide you with my protection. You, in turn, will give your service. I hope you can forgive the recent lack of leadership and set aside any harsh feelings."

Raynor scanned the crowd. "Today we make a new start. For one another. For Ashcroft!"

CHAPTER NINE

DISAPPOINTMENT FLOODED RAYNOR as silence filled the great hall. He had already failed before he'd even begun to remedy all that was wrong at Ashcroft.

Then a cheer went up and clapping workers leapt to their feet. The noise resounded throughout the room. Relief took hold of him. He raised his hands and the applause died down.

"You've cheered my words, but remember—I will ask for you to push yourselves to the limit. Winter will not wait. We must complete the harvest and make ready for the cold weather that will come."

He summoned Gobert. "Choose the five best serfs that we have. I'll meet with them now in your record room. We'll devise an immediate plan of action for today and the week to come. I also want to ride the estate afterward and see what's in need of repair, from fences to cottages. And you and I must go over the books in the near future."

"Aye, my lord." Gobert hurried off, already gesturing for others to join him.

Raynor looked down at Beatrice. "You have your work cut out for you, my lady. Start wherever you desire. Our conversation last night led me to believe you know exactly what to do."

"Trust me, my lord. I can handle all domestic matters inside the keep. I'll report to you at the end of each day on our progress."

She smiled, and for the first time he noticed the dimple in her cheek. He stopped himself from reaching out to touch it.

"Then I will leave you to your tasks," he said gruffly, tamping down the lust that burned within him. He left for the small room where the Ashcroft records were stored.

With every step, his heart pounded as if he'd been fighting for hours. Beatrice Bordel had bewitched him. Now that he'd had his first clear look at her as they returned from mass this morning, her unique beauty stunned him. Her rich, brown hair called out for his hand to stroke it. Matched in color, her warm brown eyes, rimmed in amber, danced with life. She was small in stature, yet, above all, it was her smile that had captured his heart. It reached her eyes, crinkling them in merriment.

Raynor stopped in his tracks. He couldn't meet with workers while in idle reverie over a woman, one which, he reminded himself, was promised to another. She was a guest in his home, one who had promised to help him put Ashcroft back together before he united her with her betrothed. She would add a woman's touch in areas of which he knew nothing about. Lady Beatrice would repay him for coming to her aid by helping him restore his family's home to its former glory.

Even if her mouth called out to him to be kissed.

He drew in a deep breath and expelled it slowly, trying to gain control of the wild notions running through his head. Raynor continued to the record room. He would decide how to best approach the harvest, then go to the training yard. That's where he felt most comfortable.

Minutes later, Gobert arrived with five men in tow. Raynor remembered two of them and became quickly acquainted with the other three.

"This wheat harvest is of utmost importance," he stressed. "Beginning now, we'll put in long hours each day until it's completed. Every able-bodied man, woman, and child needs to be present in the fields. If we work together, no one will starve at Ashcroft. You have my word." Raynor thought a moment. "How many scythes are there?"

John, a stout man with black hair and a thick beard, spoke up. "We have a good thirty in working condition, my lord. More, once the others are sharpened. That should happen frequently for the blades to be most effective."

"Good. Set one man to the sharpening. Rotate the tools at least once a day. The midday meal will be taken in the fields." He looked to Gobert. "Speak with Cook once we are finished here so that food and drink will be readied and taken to the workers. Have her shift the main meal to the end of the day. The same goes for the soldiers in the training yard."

The men nodded in agreement. Raynor sensed they were relieved that someone had taken charge and provided them with direction.

"You five are to have authority over the other workers. John, you shall be head of all. Divide the serfs into teams. After a week's time, we'll reorganize and allow only the men to continue with the harvest. The women and older children can begin to tie what has been collected into sheaves in order for the wheat to dry."

"My lord, I would suggest that once enough of the tying has been completed, we have men drive the carts that will transport the sheaves to be stored," John added. "Many times, the carts are filled to the brim and unsteady. They can tip over. 'Twould be too dangerous for womenfolk."

"I'll leave details such as these in your capable hands, John," Raynor said. "The same can be said for the winnowing. You may choose to start that process once enough sheaves have been transported or you may decide to wait till all of it has been gathered and brought in before the workers winnow the bundles."

He studied the men in front of him. "All of you are my eyes and ears in the field. Take care of any small problems. Bring anything of serious concern to my immediate attention. And once the wheat has been collected, tied, and winnowed, I shall hold a harvest home celebration as we did in my younger days."

Huge smiles broke out on the men's faces.

"May we share that news, my lord?" John asked eagerly.

"Aye. It will give everyone something to look forward to. Stay here and organize your teams before you head to the fields. John, you and I will meet in this room every night after we dine so that I may hear of the progress made each day."

"Aye, my lord." John looked at the other men. "We'll set the teams now and decide when to have each stage of the harvest completed."

"Good luck to you," Raynor told them. "I must check on my soldiers." He exited the room, Gobert fast on his heels.

"My lord? A word?" the steward asked.

Raynor paused, though he itched to be outside. "Aye?"

"I know it's not my place—"

"Don't stand on ceremony, Gobert. Tell me what concerns you."

The steward frowned. "It's Sir Ralph. He has grown fat and lazy. Discipline has vanished in the training yard. The men simply go through the motions. I fear Ashcroft would not survive an attack with the soldiers that we have on hand."

"I thought as much." He placed a hand on Gobert's shoulder. "Training soldiers is one thing I know about. Don't worry, my friend. Give me a few days. I promise that Ashcroft will, once again, have men worthy of protecting it."

Raynor was glad that the steward had written to him. Though much needed to be done at his family home, Raynor believed the heart of it lay with his men.

His men . . .

In truth, they were not his men. They were soldiers in service to the Baron of Ashcroft. But for now? He would claim them as his own. By the time he finished, he would be assured of Ashcroft's well-being.

When he arrived at the training yard, Raynor was stunned that only a lone knight stood in the yard. He'd told the men when he would be here and assumed they would be ready for training with their weapons in hand. Instead, he found the one soldier present, swinging his sword. The man's fluid moves and natural grace marked him as a talented warrior.

"Greetings!" he called out as he approached. "What is your name?"

"I am Sir Lucas Moore, my lord."

"You are new to Ashcroft."

"Aye, my lord. I've been here close to four months."

"And you are the only soldier who cares to train?"

The young knight started to speak and thought better of it. His gaze fell to the ground.

"Nay, speak up," Raynor prompted. "If I am to improve the circumstances, I must be well informed."

Lucas met his eyes and Raynor saw anger spark in them. "Sir Ralph has been lax in every way imaginable, my lord. The men train sporadically and with little enthusiasm. Almost half have left Ashcroft in search of a strong leader who is serious about his responsibilities."

Raynor studied the young man before him. "I appreciate your honesty, Sir Lucas. Where did you foster?"

"Outside Winchester with Lord Barrington."

"I have heard he is a hard man," Raynor said, testing the young soldier before him.

"Hard—but always fair," Lucas shared. "He never asks a man to do something that he would not do himself. I spent long hours in training, but if I had it to do over again? I would choose Lord Barrington with ease. He made me the man I am today, in every way."

"Yet you did not stay in service with him," Raynor pointed out.

"Nay. His garrison had no openings. The captain of the guard told me to seek experience as a mercenary and to send word to him where I would be. He promised to let me know if Lord Barrington had need of me in the future."

"I hope you'll choose to dedicate yourself to Ashcroft permanently, Sir Lucas. We have need of men like you."

The young knight studied him a moment. "I will stay, my lord, but only if you make the drastic changes needed."

Raynor gave Lucas a grim smile. "I can promise you that will come to pass. Immediately."

Both men turned as a group of soldiers sauntered into the training yard. Sir Ralph brought up the rear. Raynor recognized a few, but many familiar faces were missing. He assumed those were the ones who had left as things declined.

He called out, "Sir Ralph, have the men pair off. I'd like to see how they are at swordplay first."

"You should have no worries, my lord," the captain assured him. "These men are skilled fighters. I can handle the training yard. I'm sure you'll be needed to supervise the harvest. And your brother," he added.

Though his last words were uttered softly, they carried in the still of the morning.

Raynor strode toward him and slammed his fist into the man's nose. Sir Ralph stumbled and fell to the ground.

As Raynor loomed over him, he said, "You are dismissed from service, Sir Ralph. Pack your things and leave Ashcroft at once."

Turning, he looked across the soldiers gathered in the yard. "Your captain has grown careless. Slovenly ways and disrespect will never be tolerated at Ashcroft. From this moment forth, if you are to stay here, you will act as honorable men. You'll accept that your role is to protect Ashcroft and its people at all costs. You will train hard on a daily basis and present a positive attitude at all times. Most of all, you will respect the baron and pledge your loyalty to the Le Roux family. Or, you may depart with this weak, sniveling excuse of a knight."

Raynor glared at the crowd. Two fell out of the ranks and followed Sir Ralph, who'd come to his feet and stormed off. He watched them exit the training yard.

"Split into pairs," he ordered. "We'll train first with swords. Then axes and maces."

He pushed them for hours, often jumping in as a sparring partner. He judged how skilled each soldier was with various weapons. By the end of the session, sweat poured from everyone, including himself. His own limbs trembled from such intense use.

Another two men had quit during the exercises. They informed him they would leave immediately. Raynor was happy to see them go. It was easier to remove less desirable soldiers now and forge ahead with a smaller, determined crew.

Calling a halt to the activity, he pushed a forearm across his forehead to mop the sweat from his brow. He called for the men to assemble around him.

"You have done well today. I see raw talent in many of you and natural skill in many more. I'll also look for loyalty and leadership."

He gazed at the men as they listened to his words, pleased to see eagerness and determination on their faces.

"I hope you will find it an honor to serve at Ashcroft." Raynor pointed at Lucas. "Sir Lucas. Come forth."

The young knight approached.

Raynor placed a hand on the soldier's shoulder. "This man—though young in years—has the heart of a lion and fighting skills that many would envy. He is your new captain of the guard."

The knight's eyes widened at the announcement, then a huge grin spread across his face. The remaining warriors gave him a rousing cheer. Many slapped him on the back, congratulating him on a job well done. Raynor was happy to see his new captain was well liked.

"Continue with the men, Sir Lucas. I have other tasks to see to."

"As you wish, my lord."

Raynor eyed the men and said, "Keep up your hard work and you'll earn an extra measure of ale and meat tonight."

Another cheer went up.

Lucas turned to Raynor. "Thank you for your confidence in me, my lord. Not many would choose to put someone as young as I am as captain of their guard." He chuckled. "I hope you know what you are doing."

"I know exactly what I'm doing," Raynor declared. "This change will be one of my best decisions, mark my words."

CHAPTER TEN

BEATRICE'S REFUSED TO be overwhelmed with all that needed to be done inside the keep. She went to her chamber and removed the beautiful yellow cotehardie she had dressed in this morning since she didn't want it stained. For cleaning, a smock and kirtle would suffice. She met with Cook first, who provided her with an apron and showed her the location of the larder. Cook already knew what to do to prepare for the lean winter months. The stout woman seemed to be one of the few at Ashcroft who had kept about her business without the need of anyone hovering over her.

The grain stores were severely depleted. Once the wheat harvest came in and the milling occurred, though, Ashcroft would be set for bread for the next year. Salting and smoking meats would also occur during the autumn season, and hunting would pick up in earnest after the harvest had been collected. She wondered if she would still be present when that took place.

Cook showed her where the herbs were stored and Beatrice skimmed through the contents quickly. She found ample amounts of lavender and chamomile and smaller bits of fennel and rose petals that could be used to scent the fresh rushes she wanted placed in the great hall. Finding plenty of shave-grass delighted her since she'd noticed the trestle tables and benches had grown worn and rough in some spots. She even had to pick a splinter from her palm after she broke her fast this morning. If the head table was in such poor condition, she assumed the rest of the furniture in the great hall was the same. They could use the shave-grass to smooth out the oak benches and tables.

For rougher patches, they could apply the skin of a dogfish and smooth the wood using a plane and scraper to finish the job. Finding Cook again, Beatrice asked about the castle's carpenter since she would need his tools and strength to do much of the work.

"Donaldus is our carpenter," Cook informed her. "But he's in the fields with the harvesters now, my lady."

"I have need of his services. Send a servant to the fields to retrieve him."

Returning to the great hall, Beatrice gathered all of the servants that worked inside the keep. There were eight women to help her, though Cook said some would need to return to the kitchens to help prepare food later in the day. Feeding the hungry workers, especially at harvest time, took top priority.

Beatrice told them, "There'll be many tasks to carry out in order to return this room to its natural beauty. The tables and benches need smoothing. The tapestries must be removed from the walls so the dust can be beaten from them. But our first job is to clean the floor. The molding rushes. The dung. Anything you find lying on the floor must come out. Once it's gone, we'll scour the stones with soap and hot water multiple times and then wash the walls, as well."

She asked each servant for her name and designated Hilda to help organize the women and keep things running. The servants joined Beatrice as they removed every despicable piece from the floor, while Hilda saw to massive amounts of water being put on to boil. As she swept together and lifted the rotting rushes, Beatrice found herself breathing from her mouth because of the stench. Moving the heavy trestle tables away from the walls in order to reach every corner proved to be the hardest challenge for the group of women. She chastised herself, wishing she'd thought to have the men remove the furniture from the room before they left for the fields.

With so many workers involved, the floor was soon bare and the real backbreaking work began. Hilda brought in pail after pail of hot water and carted back the empties. Each woman had received a brush for scrubbing and plenty of soap. Beatrice divided the room into sections. Once a section was completed, she inspected their work before they could move on to a new area.

"My lady? You have need of me?" A bow-legged man with a scraggly beard and kind smile had entered the great hall.

"Are you Donaldus, the carpenter?" she asked.

"I am."

Beatrice explained her concern regarding the condition of the benches and trestle tables and how she wanted all bumps and ridges worked out.

"I found plenty of shave-grass. I placed it on that table in the west corner. You may use it and retrieve your plane and scraper to smooth the surfaces of every bit of furniture in the great hall."

He nodded. "I'm happy to use it. If I run out, cattails also work on oak. Sometimes, I've used rotten stone as an abrasive before I scrape and smooth. Let me retrieve my tools and I'll start at once."

"Thank you, Donaldus. It will be a nice improvement to sit and not be rewarded with a splinter in my rump."

The carpenter chuckled and excused himself.

After a few hours, more than a quarter of the stone floor had been given a thorough cleaning. Beatrice allowed the women to rest before they returned to their buckets and brushes. She sent them to the kitchens for something to eat but cautioned them to remain there. She wanted no food brought into the great hall until she was ready.

Hilda lingered after the others left. "My lady, it's time to bring the meal to the fields and the training yard. It's been the custom in the past to take the midday meal outside while the harvesting goes on. Sir Raynor has asked that we continue with this practice. Then, when dusk falls, the farm workers and soldiers will return to the great hall and dine. That's when Cook will need to borrow some of the servants to help her prepare the food."

"I'll speak to Cook, Hilda. She'll need to send the evening meal outside for the next few nights. The serfs and soldiers can eat in the bailey until the great hall has been cleaned thoroughly and the furniture completely restored. Once we've transformed the room, I think everyone will be pleased and take proper care in the future. In the meantime, while the women deliver the food to the fields, you and I can go to the herb garden so I may see what's been planted and what should be picked. We can also check the supply of rushes."

"I can show you where both are, my lady."

After seeing both places, the two women ventured back to the great hall. Beatrice noted the servants had also returned. Once again, the group of women began scrubbing the grime from the floor. They worked diligently for the rest of the afternoon, only stopping to help with the evening meal, which Beatrice had served outside.

"The people are hungry. They have put in a full day of work in the fields and the training yard," Raynor said when she joined him on the steps of the keep.

"The servants inside have done the same, my lord," Beatrice told him as she surveyed the crowd gathered as they ate their meal without conversation. "Everyone has worked diligently. We should be able to dine in a much-improved great hall soon."

She excused herself once she finished eating and returned to the bedchamber Gobert had assigned to her and fell into a dreamless sleep.

After a good night of rest, Beatrice was up and hard at work the next day, repeating the actions from the day before. It took a third day of backbreaking work before the women finished cleaning the floors and walls of the great hall to her satisfaction.

Beatrice instructed all but two of the servants to go with Hilda to retrieve fresh rushes and then assigned the two youngest girls to gather the specified herbs. Donaldus was working tirelessly. It seemed as though he'd finished with most of the furniture. If he continued at this pace, he would complete his task before night fell. The carpenter gave her a bright smile and continued scraping and whistling.

Beatrice supervised the laying of the rushes and sprinkling of the herbs atop them. It only took a few minutes with so many pitching in to spread the straw. Soon, a sweet scent filled the air. She thought to remind Raynor that no untrained dogs should be allowed in the room. She intended for these floors to remain in good condition. The people of Ashcroft would no longer live as animals.

After that, two women were sent to retrieve ladders. Once they returned, each of the four tapestries was lifted from the walls. It took the strength of every woman present to haul them outside.

"I want you to beat the life out of these tapestries," she demanded. "They look as if they haven't been cleaned in years. Hilda, please see to this and let me know when it's done. I'll be back to help you."

"Aye, my lady."

Before Beatrice turned to leave, she decided to watch as one girl lifted a stick. She gently tapped the tapestry and a small cloud of dust wafted from it.

"Nay, that won't do," she told the servant. "Give me your stick."

The girl handed it over, a hesitant look on her face.

"Step aside. Let me show you what a true cleaning involves."

Taking the stick in both hands, Beatrice whacked the tapestry as hard as she could. Dust flew from it. She struck it a few more times for good measure and stepped back, grinning in appreciation of her own work.

"That is what I ask of you. Layers of dust have settled upon the surface. These tapestries are thick and woven very tightly. I promise that you won't hurt them if you strike them hard."

Beatrice returned the borrowed stick to the girl and brushed her hands together before she wiped them on her apron.

RAYNOR LEFT THE training yard, his muscles tired from the activity of the past few hours. He'd put off riding the perimeter and inspecting the various structures on the property in order to work with the soldiers during training exercises the past few days, and he still planned to do that later today. For now, he knew it was important to go to the fields next to see how the harvesting progressed. He'd left everything in the hands of John for the past three days, allowing the worker to report to him each evening after they supped. Raynor had been pleased with what John told him, but it was time to see for himself how much the workers had already accomplished.

He came closer and saw that harvesting had come to a halt. All the serfs sat on the ground, finishing their midday meal. Raynor snatched an apple from a nearby wooden basket and munched on it as he surveyed the fields.

John came up to him. "All goes well, my lord. Everyone is cooperative and in good spirits. Much has been accomplished in the last few days."

"So, the teams are productive?"

"Aye, though I had to make an adjustment once we began. We lost Donaldus that first day."

"Donaldus? Ah, the carpenter. I remember when he made a wooden sword for me when I was a boy." Raynor smiled at the memory. "I watched every minute while he carved it. In fact, I made two myself for my cousin's children recently." He stopped. "Is Donaldus ill?"

"Nay, my lord. Lady Beatrice sent for him."

He wondered why Beatrice would need a carpenter to aid in cleaning the keep. "I think it would be better if he spent his time in the fields. I'll speak to her now and see that he returns at once."

Raynor gave John a nod of dismissal and took the last bite of his apple. He tossed the core into a basket full of them. As he returned to the main gates, he noted a man sat in the gatekeeper's perch and that two soldiers patrolled the wall-walk. It pleased him that Lucas had already implemented a schedule. He would speak with his new captain later regarding it and how the rest of the day's training had gone. Raynor wanted to be fully involved in this aspect of Ashcroft.

He made quick time through the outer and inner baileys. Both were deserted, with every available hand now dedicated to the wheat harvest. As he approached the keep, he saw a small group of women outside. They surrounded one of the tapestries from the great hall. Drawing closer, he saw a servant beating it. Dust erupted in a dark cloud around her.

Raynor was aghast when he drew closer and recognized the woman was Beatrice. She stepped back and handed the stick to a servant.

He rushed over to the group.

"Lady Beatrice!" he barked, drawing her attention—and that of every woman present.

She twirled around and he saw that she was filthy. The plain, unadorned clothing she wore was covered in dirt. Dark smudges stained her cheeks and chin. Even her hair had a covering of dust.

"Yes, my lord?" she said demurely, as if she hadn't a care in the world.

"You're not meant to do menial tasks, my lady."

Surprise crossed her face, and then she fisted her hands and brought them to her waist. "And how do you suppose things will get done, my lord? I wouldn't ask any servant here to do something that I myself am not willing to do."

Gritting his teeth, he said, "My lady, you should instruct them. *They* are the ones tasked with the activity."

"What do you think I was doing?" she asked, looking at him as if he'd gone mad. "I was demonstrating how to beat the dirt from a tapestry. They were being far too kind to the dusty weavings."

Raynor frowned. "You may tell them what they must do, but you're not to get your hands dirty in the process." He looked her up and down. "Or any of the rest of you, for that matter."

She glared up at him. "I will get my hands—*and* the rest of me—as dirty as I must in order to see that *your* family's home is brought back to a desired level of cleanliness. The job will get done better and faster if I participate." She raised her chin a notch, daring him to contradict her.

His own anger rose. "And since it's *my* family's keep and *I* have been charged to bring it back to expected standards, I *will* tell you what you can and cannot do."

Her nostrils flared. "Is that so?" She snorted in disgust. "I'm sorry to tell you, my lord, but *you* gave me authority over the domestic chores within the keep. And *I* shall do as I see fit. You told me you know nothing of these matters. Now let me get back to—"

Raynor locked his fingers around her upper arm and began leading her away from the group of servants who watched their verbal exchange with interest.

"What do you think you're doing?" she hissed, trying to escape his grasp.

"Quit being so stubborn," he whispered. "And quit causing a scene."

Beatrice stopped. She bit her lip and frowned.

He took the opportunity. "Come with me," he said softly, his tone calmer. "I would like to speak with you."

"Yes, my lord." Her words may have been compliant, but she tried to jerk her arm away again. His fingers did not budge. "Let me be."

Raynor released his hold on her. "Follow me," he ordered. He set off, not turning back to see if she followed. He only hoped she did.

As they entered the keep, he heard her footsteps on the stone floor behind him and sighed silently in relief. Leading her to the records room, he opened the door and ushered her inside.

Beatrice entered, her arms crossed over her chest. He shut the door behind him.

"Have a seat."

"I prefer to stand." She began nibbling on her bottom lip again.

Raynor refused to be driven to distraction by the gesture. He brought his hands behind him, locking his fingers together.

"You can't go against me in public, my lady," he said. "I am trying to make many changes at Ashcroft. Not everyone will be happy with what I'm doing."

She remained silent, but her gaze fell to the ground.

"We should act in harmony and present a united front to everyone. You wouldn't wish to be a bad example to the people, would you?"

Her eyes met his reluctantly. "I won't disagree with you in public," she said. "But I have a right to my opinions, you know."

"You do. And I did tell you to take full charge of the changes inside the keep. I didn't mean to question your ability in managing the servants."

"I am sorry, my lord." She sighed. "Grandfather always said I was the most stubborn person he'd ever come across. I simply want to have everything done correctly for you. If that means working alongside the others, then I must do so." She gave him a contrite smile.

He ignored the dimple flashing in her cheek. "Then I agree that we may talk in private, especially if we have a difference of opinion or if either of us has any questions. And you're right to state that you have full authority inside the keep."

"Thank you," she said. "I promise that you'll begin to see a difference, especially in the great hall tonight."

"But I would ask you to reconsider physical labor, Beatrice. Try to manage the servants instead."

Anger sparked in her eyes. "See? There you go again, telling me what to do. Raynor, it won't get done right unless I pitch in and become one of many hands at Ashcroft. I'm not some delicate flower. I may be small, but I'm strong."

Beatrice stepped back and took a seat. He saw that she trembled.

"I am the one who cooked all the meals in our manor house and cleaned it from top to bottom. I gathered the eggs and fed the animals. Well, all but our horse," she admitted. "I sewed our clothes and mended them when they needed repair and tended my ill mother, all with no servant to help me. I'm not a stranger to hard work because I've done it all my life."

She flushed a deep red. She had gotten quite worked up. He crossed to her chair and knelt beside her. He wiped a smudge of dirt from her cheek with his thumb. Her fair skin was softer than the down on a newborn's head.

Without thinking, he narrowed the distance between them and put his lips upon hers.

CHAPTER ELEVEN

THE ANGER THAT coursed through Beatrice stopped as Raynor pressed his mouth to hers. His scent, a mix of leather and sweat, filled her senses. Her arms fell limply to her sides as his lips brushed softly against hers, calling out to her. She opened her mouth to reply and found his tongue slipping inside. It began running along her own tongue, teasing and drawing away and then returning in a game she hadn't known existed.

But one she was more than ready to play.

Instinctively, her arms rose and locked around his neck, pulling him closer. He responded by wrapping his hands about her waist, lifting her from the chair as if she weighed no more than a feather.

Beatrice leaned into his hard, muscled chest, taking in his heat. His tongue continued to plunder her mouth until her mind was void of any thought but this moment. Tingles of pleasure rippled through her. Large hands splayed against her back, spanning it.

And still he kissed her.

'Twas almost more than she could bear. Her insides melted like snow did in spring. Her knees weakened. She held on to him tightly, afraid to let go, afraid he would stop. A low moan echoed in the room, and Beatrice realized that it came from her. An intense longing for something she didn't understand but wished to lay claim to spread through her.

Suddenly, she found herself back in the chair from where she had started this journey. Raynor had put her there. He took a few steps away from her, looking confused.

Something had happened that baffled him. Had he felt the same intense feelings she'd experienced? What did they mean?

He opened his mouth, but nothing came out. Staring at her with hunger, he merely shook his head before he took another step back.

"My . . . my lady," he whispered, his voice low and hoarse. "I . . . am . . ."

The knight struggled to find words. She longed to reach out and touch him. Beatrice wanted to stroke his cheek. She needed to place her head against his chest and listen to his beating heart.

Raynor finally found his voice. "I am sorry for the distress I've caused you," he said brusquely. "It will not happen again. I give you my solemn oath."

Before she could reply, he left the room, slamming the door behind him.

Beatrice brought her fingertips to her lips, touching where his mouth had been locked against hers. Everything she had ever thought she'd known had shifted as sands did when the tide rolled in and out. No longer did she feel simply indebted to this knight, thankful that he'd rescued her and brought her to the safety of his family's home. Instead, Beatrice acknowledged the growing attraction to him stirring inside her—something that could be dangerous to act upon.

She realized now why such a look of concern had crossed Raynor's face. He thought he'd violated his code of chivalry. Knights were sworn to protect the honor of women. By kissing her, Raynor had betrayed her trust in him and taken advantage of a betrothed woman. Beatrice longed to run after him and explain that she was unattached. She wanted to tell Raynor that she cared for him and was free to return any feelings he might have for her, for surely the knight's kiss told her he also sensed the connection developing between them.

But how could he trust her after she had lied to him?

A river of hot tears came and she thought she might be sick. She wanted to curl up and die from humiliation and loneliness.

Then the practical woman she'd long been forced her tears to subside. Of course, she didn't want to die. She was young and had many years of life ahead of her. Her grandfather would have been ashamed of the way she'd behaved.

A few nights ago on the road, though, she could have lost her life. The highwaymen who'd ransacked their cart had killed Tolly and they could easily have killed her, as well. Beatrice was alive—thanks to good fortune bringing Raynor Le Roux her way at a critical moment. Raynor deserved an honest woman with an ample dowry, not a penniless liar such as herself.

Beatrice decided that she must act as a knight on a mission and repay the Le Roux family for the kindness Raynor had shown to her, a complete stranger. When done, the keep would shine. It would be a place that Raynor, his brother, and all the people of Ashcroft would be proud to live.

More importantly, her longings would remain unspoken. She would not encourage Raynor Le Roux in any way. It didn't matter that his kiss made her feel utterly feminine. No more dwelling on his beautiful, green eyes and burnished hair. She'd ignore his towering, muscled frame and, when the time came, allow him to escort her north to Brookhaven.

Most importantly, Beatrice would never let him see her cry again.

She composed herself and then returned, unseen, to her chamber where she washed her face with cool water before she headed to the great hall.

As she expected, the women had finished with the tapestries. They had borrowed Donaldus from his duties so he could climb the ladder. With the women's help, he hung the third of the four tapestries. She watched from the doorway as the final one was put into place.

"You've done excellent work today," Beatrice praised. She was happy to see the pleased looks upon the servants' faces. "Hilda, take two of the women to the herb garden. Have them pick the herbs we discussed earlier. The rest of you may return to the kitchen to help Cook. She'll have need of you in preparing the evening meal. The workers coming in from the fields will be hungry. Tonight, we will all gather in the great hall for our evening meal."

"What's next, my lady?" Hilda asked.

"I plan to spend the rest of this afternoon touring the keep. I'll note what is stored and what should be replenished, then visit the occupied chambers to see what should be done in them. Those will be our first priorities, then we can work on the empty rooms. We can meet after we break our fast tomorrow. You'll receive your duties then."

Beatrice watched as Hilda selected two women for the herb gathering from the garden, while the rest returned to the kitchens. Donaldus had already gone back to work on the furniture. She decided to see how far he had gotten.

"How do you fare, Donaldus?"

"Right well, my lady. 'Twere only a few places that needed to be evened out today. I should be finished in the next hour or two."

"I appreciate your hard work," she told him.

The carpenter laughed. "And I appreciate even more that you asked me to work with my tools. Harvesting is hard. All that bending and swinging of the scythes. You saved my poor back, at least for these past few days. I shall return to the fields tomorrow."

"Do you believe the benches and trestle tables are in good condition then? Or do new ones need to be built instead?"

He cocked his head in thought. "It would be wise to replace some, though most are fine. Oak is a durable wood."

"Then I would prefer you start work tomorrow by crafting the replacements. And I may find more for you to do once I have toured the keep."

Donaldus gave her a quick nod. "With pleasure, my lady. I much prefer working with wood any day." He frowned. "Are you sure Sir Raynor will agree to this? He said every able-bodied man should be in the field."

"If he truly meant that, then he would have sent all those soldiers there to help. Don't worry. You're excused from the harvest. If you finish what I need done, only then will you rejoin the serfs in the field."

"Aye, my lady." The carpenter bent his head and returned to the bench before him.

Satisfied with the progress made in the great hall, Beatrice climbed the stairs to the top of the keep. She found a turret room that seemed unused, with thick layers of dust covering every surface. She shook her head at its horrible condition, wondering why Raynor's brother hadn't been a more reliable baron. Why hadn't the nobleman married again? Why did he vanish for days on end, not living up to his responsibilities?

If the roles were reversed, she believed Raynor would never have let the estate fall into such disrepair.

Beatrice descended the stairs and viewed the next floor's chambers. It soon became apparent that no one occupied any room on this floor, so she proceeded to the next level. This was where she stayed. Beatrice investigated each room carefully and knew instantly when she came upon the one Raynor had slept in the night before because his scent filled the air.

Walking around the room, the smell was uniquely his. She paused in the center of the chamber and closed her eyes and relived their kisses.

One had led to another—and another—as he took command of her mouth. Just the memory of his body next to hers, his lips on hers, their tongues swirling, mating, brought back a deep sense of satisfaction.

And desire.

Being in Raynor's presence was the first time she'd experienced male companionship. She opened her eyes, marveling over the surge of new feelings she'd experienced in his presence. The knight continually occupied her thoughts. She could hear his hearty laugh. Feel his strong, calloused hand as it covered hers. Taste his essence. See his chiseled cheeks and piercing green eyes.

Beatrice stomped her foot in frustration. Raynor would most likely avoid her after what had happened between them and only speak to her when necessary. He'd do his duty and see that she journeyed north to Sir Henry's, but he would never kiss her again. His knightly code would see to that. Yet, a part of her wondered if he would feel differently knowing she had no betrothed awaiting her at Brookhaven.

For a moment, Beatrice gave in and imagined telling him the news and seeing his reaction, picturing the look of disappointment as he watched her. Raynor Le Roux was a man marked by honor. He would not look lightly upon her lies, no matter the reason behind them.

And when had she become such a liar? She had written a falsehood to Sir Henry Stollers when she told him that she and her grandfather would soon visit him. She had lied to Amfrid and told him she had a future husband who would pay for the return of her mother's necklace. Then she misled Raynor into believing she would soon be married. It frightened her that these lies would soon catch up to her. Though she couldn't recollect ever telling a lie before, now her life seemed to be made up of nothing but untruths. Even if she'd done it to protect herself, she didn't recognize the woman she'd become.

Beatrice lifted a tunic the color of rust from Raynor's bed. She brought it to her nose and inhaled as she held it against her and stroked it. This was as close as she would ever get to him. The thought brought a stab of pain to her. She quickly placed the tunic on the bed again and thoroughly inspected the bedchamber, deciding what must be done to make it clean again. After that, she visited the remaining rooms on the floor, finding most of them in similar shape.

Then she reached what had to be the solar. The manor house she'd grown up in did not have one due to its smaller size, but vague memories of the solar in the castle where she'd been born flashed in her mind. She knocked on the closed door, wondering if the Baron of Ashcroft might be inside since Raynor said his brother had returned, though she hadn't caught sight of him. No one answered, so Beatrice pushed the door open.

The large room had a high ceiling. A long table with benches on each side sat in the center of the room. This would be where the family could retire for a more intimate meal. Other chairs and small tables were scattered about. A chess set rested upon one of them. Picking up a rook, she found the playing piece covered in a layer of dust. Obviously, no one had played any games for some time.

She crossed to another closed door and knocked, doubting anyone was inside. Opening it, she discovered the largest bedchamber in the entire keep. Even if she had put the three bedchambers at the manor house together, they would have fit inside this one with room to spare.

Beatrice walked to the bed and drew back the curtains and fingered the bedclothes. Though worn, they seemed clean. The pillows needed to be replaced, as did the curtains, but she could tell someone cleaned the solar on a regular basis.

"Who are you?" a voice demanded.

Startled, Beatrice turned and found a man standing in the doorway, his face in shadows. He stepped forward, looking unkempt, wearing tattered clothing, and sporting an untrimmed beard.

No one needed to tell her that Peter Le Roux stood before her. The baron was a pale shadow of Raynor, different in many ways. Though tall, he was still shorter than his younger brother. Lord Peter was also thin, where Raynor was muscled. Still, the baron had the Le Roux skin and hair. Despite his angry tone, his eyes appeared dull and lifeless. They had none of the spark of fun and mischief that Raynor's possessed.

Beatrice curtsied to him. "Lord Peter. I am pleased to make your acquaintance. I am Lady Beatrice Bordel. Your—"

He marched toward her and captured her upper arms in his hands, his fingers digging into the tender flesh. "I don't care who you are. What are doing in my bedchamber, dragging in your filth?"

She glanced down and saw how soiled her clothing had become from beating the dust from the tapestries. "I am . . . that is . . . Sir Raynor brought me here. He came—"

"He dares to bring one of his whores here? And you enter my solar, where . . . my beloved wife . . ." His voice cracked. He flung her aside.

Beatrice stumbled back, the edge of the bed prevented her from falling. This nobleman's violence caused her temper to flare.

She stood tall and faced him. "I am no leman, my lord," she proclaimed. "Sir Raynor saved my life several nights ago. I was accosted by highwaymen who killed my servant. Sir Raynor brought me to safety here at Ashcroft. And though he spoke fondly of his home, even I could see his embarrassment at what this place has become."

The nobleman's eyes widened in surprise. Beatrice knew not to speak to a lord in such a rude manner, but she couldn't stop herself.

"The great hall stank of piss and dung and rotting food. Your soldiers are lax and undisciplined. The autumn harvest has barely begun. *You* were nowhere to be found."

Beatrice shook a finger at him. "You should be ashamed of what you haven't done. How you've left your people struggling. Sir Raynor has organized the serfs and begun the harvest in earnest. He's met the men in the training yard and is making sure your soldiers will protect Ashcroft. To repay him for saving my life, I told him I would help make improvements inside the keep. *That* is why I am in your chamber, my lord. I've been to every room in order to see what must be done to restore Ashcroft to a clean and comfortable home. Once I've completed my tasks and the harvest is collected, I'll be gone from your sight."

Lord Peter sucked in a breath.

Beatrice pushed on, this time softening her tone. "Aye, I know you lost a wife and your precious newborn. No man should have to face such sorrow. But the people of Ashcroft depend upon you, my lord. Your brother depends upon you. Rouse yourself from your stupor and be the baron that they need."

Beatrice folded her arms against her protectively, suddenly afraid she'd gone too far. This nobleman could have her severely punished for simply raising her voice to him. She bit her lip to still the trembling of her mouth. Her defiance died as her temper cooled.

Peter Le Roux closed his mouth and studied her for some time. Then he said, "You are the woman I have been waiting for, Beatrice Bordel. The one who would wake me from this living death."

He closed the gap between them and placed his hands upon her shoulders.

"I want to take you to wife."

CHAPTER TWELVE

RAYNOR FINISHED RIDING the border around Ashcroft. After he'd fled Beatrice's company, he had spent the rest of the afternoon on Fury, touring the remaining parts of the estate he hadn't seen since his return home. Already, he noted that the storage barn needed shoring up, as did the hen house. He found numerous places in the fence that needed mending. Soon, he would take more time to thoroughly examine the cottages where the workers lived, but first he would address these more pressing repairs.

Raynor climbed down from Fury and began to pace, thoughts swirling through his mind. He'd always found comfort in movement. Striding across the meadow, he looked to the castle in the distance. In the silence, he reflected on what he'd deliberately pushed from his thoughts all afternoon.

That kiss.

From the moment his mouth touched hers, he knew that it was a mistake—yet that awareness hadn't stopped him from plundering the rich sweetness of her. Raynor had kissed his share of women.

None had the effect on him that Lady Beatrice Bordel did.

With Beatrice in his arms, Raynor had felt as if he could conquer the world. He came alive as never before, unmitigated awareness coursing through his veins.

Yet, he feared he would never have her because she belonged to another. For that reason alone, he would miss out on the life he'd always dreamed of.

He pulled the ever-present blue garter from his pocket, the one he had removed from Merryn's leg on the day of her wedding to Geoffrey. Geoffrey had told his bride that his cousin would give the keepsake to a special woman one day, one that Raynor would swear to love and be faithful to always. More than anything, he wanted the garter to belong to Beatrice.

Raynor knew it was foolish to dwell on such a hopeless situation. She was an innocent and a betrothed woman. Above all, he was a knight of the realm, pledged to support his king, honor women, and dedicating himself to God. If he compromised Beatrice's reputation and became derelict in his oath, he would be worthless.

As he paced, Raynor remembered that he had neglected to send a messenger to Sir Henry Stollers. What greeted him upon his arrival at Ashcroft had driven the thought away. So much about his home still had to be addressed, yet Raynor needed to let the nobleman know that Beatrice was safe and that he would escort her to Brookhaven in due time for her wedding.

He toyed with the idea of sending her to Brookhaven tomorrow in the company of others, but who could he rely on to protect her during such a long journey? At this point, few men in the soldiers' ranks had gained his trust. It was important for those men to remain at Ashcroft in order to aid him as he trained a new force to protect the castle and its inhabitants. It was up to him to lead the castle's knights and soldiers by example. Leaving now to take Beatrice north wasn't a choice.

Raynor also knew Beatrice to be an honorable woman. She would feel an obligation to repay the debt she believed she owed him. Even if he insisted she leave in the morning, she would be stubborn enough to defy him and demand to stay until Ashcroft was returned to its former days.

Stopping in his tracks, he knew what he must do—push aside his romantic feelings. After all, he would only see her briefly in the mornings at mass and while they broke their fast. They would attend to separate duties throughout the day.

Only at night, when they dined together, would he have to spend much time in her company. The thought of sharing a trencher tore at his gut. He swore then and there never to be alone with her again. When they were thrown together in the company of others, he would keep their conversation light and only speak of inconsequential matters.

He would need to approach the situation as if he marched into battle. Just as he armed his body with protective armor to repel his enemies, he must now arm his heart against letting Beatrice into it any deeper.

Raynor mounted his horse, determined to hold fast to his plan.

"YOU WISH TO . . . marry me?"

Shock reverberated through Beatrice. This nobleman wanted to *wed* her? For a brief moment, she considered it, tempted by how it could change everything.

She had no home and no one to protect her. She had only a few gold coins that wouldn't last for long. She would soon embark upon a journey to the estate of a man she had never laid eyes upon. If Sir Henry had no need of her—or outright rejected her—her future was one of uncertainty.

Dare she consider this rash offer of marriage from a stranger?

Marrying Peter Le Roux could solve all of her existing problems. She would have a roof over her head, as well as a titled husband that would bring her instant respect. If lucky, even friendship might grow between them.

Or mayhap . . . *love*.

That thought jarred her from the fantasy she wove. For if she married Peter Le Roux, she would wed a pale shadow of Raynor—the man who held her heart.

And what would it be like when Raynor took a wife? Naturally, he would bring her to live at Ashcroft. Beatrice would be expected to befriend the woman while she saw her interact with her husband each day. Beatrice would watch as they shared a trencher at every meal. She would see when Raynor stole a kiss from his new bride when he thought no one was looking. And she would be heartsick when the couple mounted the stairs at night, knowing another woman warmed his bed and birthed his children.

Beatrice could never live that way. Starving would be preferable over having another piece of her die each day as she watched the man she loved make a new life with another woman.

But it meant perpetuating the lie she had told—the seemingly innocent lie that she'd used to protect herself when a passing stranger came out of the dark and rescued her that night in the forest. She needed to add to it in order to convince Peter Le Roux from pressing his suit.

Searching the face of the man who had just offered for her hand, Beatrice chose her words carefully.

"My lord, I am flattered to receive this proposal of marriage from you. 'Twould be an honor to become your baroness and raise fine sons and daughters here at Ashcroft. I wish I could accept, but I fear I cannot."

Puzzlement crossed his features. "Why not? I am in good health. I have no wife, as you pointed out. Ashcroft is in need of a woman with a steady hand and sharp eye." He smiled and she saw his white, even teeth. "Surely, my lady, you could work wonders with not only the castle, but with me." He gave her a wider smile and, again, she could see the ghost of Raynor within him.

"I cannot wed you because I am promised to another. Betrothed," she said more firmly, using the word that would put an end to him seeking her out. "I was traveling to Sir Henry Stollers' estate in the north when I was accosted by highwaymen. Sir Henry was my grandfather's oldest, dearest friend. He has a grandson close to my age and we are to be married in three months' time."

There. She'd said it. It would take hours of prayers asking for forgiveness from the Virgin Mary for such a grievous sin—but at least it would end the baron's pursuit of her.

The nobleman's hands fell from her shoulders in defeat. "I see," he said quietly.

"If you'll excuse me, my lord, I still have much to attend to."

Beatrice fled the bedchamber. She paused in the corridor. Her heart raced and her knees trembled. More than that, her head pounded something fierce. She leaned her forehead against the cool stones of the wall and closed her eyes, her thoughts whirling.

Had she made a grave mistake? Should she have accepted Peter Le Roux's sudden offer? Could she have learned to live with him, while she watched Raynor with another woman?

No.

She resigned herself to spending another few weeks at Ashcroft in Raynor's company, longing for him every day. He would accompany her to the north and Beatrice would never see the knight again. Every day of her life would be full of misery.

How had she gotten into such a mess?

If only she could have defended herself and Tolly from those highwaymen. Mayhap, then the two of them would still be on the road toward Brookhaven. Raynor Le Roux would never have stopped and come to her aid. She would never have known the warmth of his arms. The concern that filled those green eyes.

The kisses he had bestowed upon her.

Beatrice would never have known any of it, for they never would have met. Or if he had come upon them as she vanquished the robbers, they would have exchanged a few brief words before going their separate ways.

She knew now what she would ask of Raynor when she next saw him.

Returning downstairs, she asked for hot water to be brought to her chamber. The servants arrived and also gave her a cake of scented soap. As she scrubbed the filth from her body, the scent of roses wafted about her. She dried herself and dressed carefully in a different *cotehardie*. This one was the color of warmed gold and fit her better than her earlier choice had.

As she descended the stairs, the noise coming from the great hall let her know the evening meal would be served soon.

When she walked through the large room, a hush settled over the hall. Beatrice smiled with satisfaction as she approached the dais, knowing the many days of toil were appreciated by those who gathered inside.

Raynor stood to greet her and offered her a hand to help her up. They seated themselves on the bench.

"My lady, I must compliment you on the miracle you have wrought in the great hall. My spirits were lifted to enter and smell the sweet scent of fresh rushes and see the clean floor." He brushed his hand over the smoothed tabletop. "And I can even feel the difference in the table before us. If this were the only contribution you made during your visit, 'twould be more than enough."

"I hope those present appreciate it as much as you do, my lord."

He waved a hand through the air. "Look about, my lady. Your efforts have been noted."

Beatrice glanced across the room and knew his words to be true by the happy expressions on the faces of the people.

"It's a good start, but I have much more to complete in my time here."

A passing servant poured each of them wine. She gave a hesitant smile as Beatrice thanked her.

"How did you fare in the herb garden?" Beatrice asked, recognizing the girl as one of the servants Hilda had taken with her to collect herbs.

"Very well, my lady. I hope you'll be pleased with what we picked."

"Would you like my help in drying and pressing what was collected?"

The girl's eyes lit up. "That I would."

"After we break our fast tomorrow, we'll work together."

The servant bobbed her head and left.

"So, you delegated the task of picking herbs?"

Beatrice caught the teasing light in Raynor's eye. "I did, my lord. I had other tasks to carry out. I examined each of the chambers in the keep and made note of what should be done. Not everything may be finished before I depart from Ashcroft, but I should make a good start on my list."

A shadow crossed his face as she referred to her departure. She decided to address what had occurred between them before he did. Beatrice believed there was no sense in letting it brew and fester.

"My lord, you know I am beholden to you for your help. I was in a dire situation when you came across me and I appreciate that you brought me back to Ashcroft with you." She paused. "I hope that we can become friends while I'm here. That nothing which occurred today will keep us from becoming so."

A muscle twitched in his cheek. "I would like that, my lady."

"I hope that things will not be awkward between us because of—"

"My ungallant behavior," he said. He looked at her earnestly. "I can't apologize enough for my untoward actions. I pray you will find it in your heart to forgive me."

"There is nothing to forgive," she said softly. "I was as much a participant in those kisses as you were, my lord." She swallowed and then pressed on. "But I hope that will not keep us at a distance during my stay at Ashcroft or when we journey to Brookhaven."

Raynor smiled. Beatrice noted it was tinged with sadness. "Then if you're willing, so am I. Let's put the unfortunate incident behind us. I promise to keep my knightly vows in mind, and I would welcome the chance to become friends during your stay in my family's home."

She lifted her pewter goblet. "To friendship."

He did the same. "To friendship."

They touched their cups together, but how Beatrice wished they had touched lips instead. Though she told Raynor she wished for friendship, what she longed for was something more. Knowing that could never be, she would treasure any time spent in his company. She would lock the memory of them away for now and then take it out to savor over the years to come.

Hoping to gather some courage, she downed a huge swallow of wine and set her cup on the table. "I have a request of you."

Raynor frowned. "Is something amiss? What can I do to correct the matter?"

"Nay, all is well. I simply have need of your skills. I... what I mean is... I would like to learn to fight. To protect myself. I know you can show me how to do so."

He looked surprised. "But I am here, my lady. You have no need to learn to protect yourself. 'Tis what I—and every other man—should do for you."

Beatrice shook her head. "Nay, I do want to learn. You will look after me here and on the road. But I'll be left at Brookhaven where I don't know a soul." She took another sip of the wine. "I found myself at a terrible disadvantage when accosted by those highwaymen. I keep telling myself that if I could have stood up to them, Tolly might still be alive."

"I doubt that. 'Twas three of them to your one."

"Still," she pleaded, "I wish to learn how to defend myself. I beg of you to teach me. Oh, I know I'm not strong enough to wield a sword. But mayhap if I had a small dagger. Or if I knew how to fend off an attacker so I could protect myself and those around me."

Raynor laughed.

"I am serious, my lord."

He held back a smile. "I know you are. All right. I'll do as you ask. I'll teach you a few tricks. I'll find a baselard that you can keep on you and instruct you in how to use it. If that will make you feel better, then I am at your disposal."

Beatrice relaxed, happy to have him honor her request. She still felt guilty over not having been able to save Tolly. She would take to heart whatever Raynor taught her and hope she never had to use it.

"Greetings, Lady Beatrice. Brother."

Her head jerked up at the words. Peter Le Roux stood before them. Gone was the disheveled man she had met earlier this afternoon. The baron had shaved and wore new clothing. She noticed the resemblance between the brothers more now, but Raynor still outshone his brother in every way.

"Good evening, Peter," Raynor said. "I am glad you could join us. I would like you to meet—"

"No need for introductions, Raynor. I have met the bewitching lady." He swept a hand across as he looked out over the room. "And I now bear witness to the transformation of the great hall at her hands."

Peter turned and gave Beatrice a knowing smile. "I believed you could work wonders and so you have."

"Where did you meet?" Raynor asked.

"In my bedchamber."

Raynor leapt to his feet.

"I saved the solar for last as I toured the keep this afternoon. I was deciding how to freshen up the room when Lord Peter entered, and I introduced myself to him," she said quickly.

Humor sparkled in Peter's eyes. "Aye, Lady Beatrice certainly put me in my place."

Beatrice's cheeks burned. "I am sorry, my lord. I did not mean to offend you."

"Oh, I think you fully intended to insult me. Even jolt me into action." He shrugged. "It did the trick. After my conversation with Lady Beatrice, I am a new man."

"You certainly look more like the brother I once knew," Raynor noted as he sat again. "I'm happy you've come to the great hall for the evening meal. The people need to see you."

"Aye, Lady Beatrice chastised me for that, as well. She let me know how derelict I'd become in my duties. I intend to change all that."

Peter's eyes lingered on her. He came to sit on her other side. She was now dwarfed by the Le Roux brothers and felt quite small.

The same servant from before rushed over and brought a cup of wine for the baron. He nodded his thanks as she scurried off.

"Tell me, Brother, when do you plan to escort the lady north?"

"In a few weeks, Peter. I want to see that the harvest is in good shape and that the soldiers are, once more, a disciplined unit. Why?"

"I wish to accompany you on this journey."

"Why would you choose to do so?" Raynor asked.

"Because I have decided to marry Lady Beatrice. I'll need to see about breaking the marriage contract with her betrothed."

CHAPTER THIRTEEN

ANGER FLOODED RAYNOR—as well as jealousy—for not having thought to do the same. "Are you mad, Peter?"

Beatrice sprang to her feet, her eyes downcast and her face beet red. "Excuse me, my lords." She lifted her skirts and raced from the great hall as if the room had caught fire.

Raynor watched her go and then faced his brother. "I demand to know why you wish to pursue the lady."

Peter's features softened. "She is like no other woman I've ever met. I'd grown discontented these past few years. I had no interest in my life or those around me. Yet, one encounter with Lady Beatrice altered my perspective. She spoke to me as no one has dared to, calling me out for my lack of leadership. Suddenly, I could clearly see all the possibilities and opportunities available to me because of her words."

His voice dropped. "It's odd to even say this, but she made me want to be a better man. For her. For those around me. And for myself."

Raynor knew what Peter meant because he felt exactly the same.

He placed a hand on his brother's shoulder. "I have not known her long, but I do know that she is a principled woman, Peter. Her parents are deceased. She is to go to her husband-to-be. I'm happy to have the brother back I've missed, but I beg of you. Don't force her into an awkward situation. Let her journey to Brookhaven and meet her obligations there when she arrives."

When his brother didn't speak, Raynor squeezed Peter's shoulder. "She is as good as married because of her betrothal. You must not try to force her union to be dissolved on a whim."

Peter threw off his hand. "My feelings for Lady Beatrice are not merely a whim." His eyes narrowed. "If I cannot have her, I want no other woman. Do you hear me? I want to be left alone!" The baron's angry outburst drew the eyes of everyone present as he stormed from the great hall.

Raynor understood his brother's dilemma, but he would do his duty and fulfill his promise to escort Beatrice to Sir Henry's and leave her in good hands.

And then? Raynor would never divorce himself from the world as Peter had, though he knew no joy would be found without Beatrice in his life.

A servant served his meal without comment. He realized that Beatrice had left before eating. As he ate a few bites, the food tasted like sand in his mouth. Raynor decided to take the meal to her. She had labored long and hard today and needed to eat in order to keep up her strength. Motioning a servant over, he asked for a tray of food he could take upstairs.

Within minutes, it was ready for him. Raynor slipped from the great hall and carried the tray to her bedchamber. He hesitated to knock, afraid he would find her in tears. Poor Beatrice had been through so much since he'd stumbled upon her.

Rapping on the door, he received no answer. He knocked harder a second time. Still, she didn't come to the door. Concerned, he stepped inside the chamber.

Beatrice was seated in a chair by the only window. She'd combed her hair out and seemed lost in thought as she hummed softly to herself. Her beauty humbled him and he didn't know what to say.

He had tender feelings for this woman and truly admired her spirit and quick temper. Raynor's gut wrenched painfully. The temptation of Beatrice Bordel dangling before him like forbidden fruit, forever unable to touch her, nearly brought Raynor to his knees.

She spotted him.

"Are you well?" he asked, closing the door behind him. "I must apologize for my brother's strange behavior. He truly hasn't been himself since he lost his wife and child."

"I promise you, my lord, that I didn't encourage Lord Peter in any way. I'm confused how this came about. One minute, I lost my temper and chastised him for his neglect of Ashcroft and its people. The next, he asked for my hand in marriage."

She stood, distress marring her lovely features. "I explained to him that I was betrothed. He must be mad to think Sir Henry would consider breaking the marriage contract." She paused. "I don't want him on our journey north, my lord. I cannot have him barge into Brookhaven demanding to set aside the contract. Can you see to that?"

"I already have," Raynor assured her as he fought the urge to take her into his arms and kiss her senseless. More than anything, he wished to be the man who stormed into Brookhaven and demanded the contract be cancelled so they could find the nearest priest and get married, then consummate their union.

Yet, what did he have to offer Beatrice? Nothing. Peter was the Baron of Ashcroft, holding both the land and title. Even if, by some miracle, Raynor could break the betrothal contract and Beatrice was free to marry him, how could he bring her back to Ashcroft and flaunt their marriage before his brother? Nothing would be more uncomfortable than having Peter constantly watch Beatrice as a hungry cat did a mouse.

Raynor worried about Peter's instability. The swings from isolating himself for long spells to this wild talk of sweeping aside Beatrice's betrothal and marrying her—then proclaiming he wanted to be left alone again. Mayhap Beatrice did need to learn how to protect herself. He couldn't be by her side all the time. What if Peter came across her and forced himself upon her? Though the thought pained him, Raynor realized he no longer trusted his brother.

Raising the tray he carried, he said, "I brought you something to eat." He placed it on a nearby table. "And I haven't forgotten your request. We should arrange a time for your lessons."

Before he could suggest they start immediately, Beatrice yawned.

Tonight wasn't the time to teach her how to defend herself after such a long, tiring day.

"I'll be working with the men in the training yard all day tomorrow. I've invited soldiers from a neighboring estate to spar with us two days from now. I must make sure Ashcroft's soldiers are prepared and can best Lord Harper's men."

"What about after that, my lord?" she asked.

"That's when we'll make time for your instruction. I know your days have been busy, but surely you can set aside an hour for me. Plan on it in three days' time. You can eat a light meal at midday and then we can meet afterward. It won't take long to show you a few ways to defend yourself, even without the use of a weapon."

Beatrice rewarded him with a sweet smile. "Very well. I shall be happy for you to tutor me then."

Raynor drank in one last look. "Good night, my lady."

He left her, knowing that she would remain with him in his dreams that night.

BEATRICE WAS PLEASED with how productive the morning had been. Many of the herbs collected over the past few days had been dried, labeled, and stored. She'd left two servants to finish the job and had gone to supervise the candle making with the remaining women. It would take the rest of today and another one to finish up that task since the Ashcroft supply was dangerously low. Once completed, she would have all the servants begin work on cleaning the occupied chambers.

She caught sight of Raynor standing in the doorway of the great hall and signaled for him to go upstairs since today had been designated for her defense lessons. Beatrice charged Hilda with directing the women while she was gone and then proceeded to follow Raynor, who waited for her at the top of the staircase.

"I'd rather we work without others watching," she told him. "I don't wish it to be known what I attempt."

"I agree. The training yard is the last place you need to be. Your beauty would be a distraction to the soldiers. If we ventured out to the training yard, the men wouldn't be able to concentrate on their maneuvers."

Beatrice tried to brush aside her embarrassment.

"There are two empty chambers down the hall we can use," she told him.

She led them to the larger of the two. Raynor closed the door behind them.

"Did you bring a dagger for me?" she asked. "I am eager to learn how to use one."

He chuckled. "We will save weapons for another day. I will show you many things you can do to ward off a man."

He pointed to his face. "A man is most vulnerable 'round his eyes and nose. If you feel threatened, you must strike quickly to weaken him. As for you, my lady, your weapons will be your elbows, knees, and forehead, for they are stronger than you know."

Raynor closed the gap between them. "If you are seated next to a man and believe you are in danger, stiffen your neck." He knelt down so he was closer to her in height.

Beatrice did as he asked. "But what good will this do, my lord?"

"Drive your forehead into the center of my face. Not with force, but try it slowly."

She kept her neck taut and as if nodding, tilted her head back and then lowered her forehead down to his nose. The minute they connected, she felt a quickening of her heart and drew back.

"Your forehead is very sturdy," he continued, "whereas, a nose is not. If you slam your forehead into your enemy's nose, he won't expect a vigorous blow, least of all from a woman. He'll find it difficult to act, especially if you've broken it. Try it again, as before."

She repeated the motion several times, bringing her forehead down against his nose until she felt comfortable with the movement. Raynor praised her effort.

"If a man clutches his broken nose, then it's time for you to run. In fact, anytime you strike a blow, my best advice is to lift your skirts and dash away while your attacker is incapacitated."

He cupped her face with his large hands. Beatrice held her breath in anticipation, thinking he was about to kiss her again.

Instead, he turned his thumbs and brought them toward her eyes. She flinched and closed her lids as his thumbs gently rested atop them. They remained that way until he removed them.

Beatrice opened her eyes, puzzled.

"Now do the same to me."

She raised her hands to his face and repeated what he had done. As the pads of her thumbs covered his eyelids, Raynor said, "You can blind a man if you gouge his eyes out."

She squealed and yanked her hands away. "Nay! I cannot do that!"

He laughed. "Your safety is what is important, my lady. If you fear for your life, you must go for his eyes. What does it matter if an attacker can no longer see you? You must do whatever it takes to protect yourself."

Beatrice understood that Raynor was only trying to help her, though she doubted she would ever be able to carry through with such violence. "How else might I protect myself, my lord?" she asked.

Raynor thought a moment. "If you are near enough, you many punch a man's throat. It is a certain way to render him powerless." He took her hands in his, causing a ripple of heat to travel down her arms.

"Place your thumb here, against my Adam's apple. This is the very spot you would hit."

Beatrice removed her fingers from his throat. She wished she could place them on it again. This time, she would stroke it lovingly. She shook her head and told herself to concentrate as Raynor began to speak again.

"Another sensitive spot on a man is his groin."

Her eyes flew to his.

"I would suggest thrusting your knee into it as hard as you can. A man will double over. In fact, while he's bent over, lift your knee high and smash it into his nose. He won't know where to comfort himself."

"Then run," she added.

"Yes," he smiled. "Try it. Slowly."

Raynor had her practice the move several times. She swung her knee toward him and then pretended to smash his nose as before, her cheeks flaming.

"Excellent. Now turn around," he instructed.

Beatrice did as he asked. Raynor wrapped himself about her, his left arm going firmly around her waist while his right hand covered her mouth. He yanked her tightly against him.

Her insides lit up. Need throbbed between her thighs.

His lips grazed her ear, and she shivered uncontrollably.

"If you're pinned in such a way where you cannot use your arms or scream and draw attention to yourself, then stomp your heel into your attacker's foot. Try it."

Beatrice heard his words, but she found it hard to react.

"I know," he said when she failed to move. "Being trapped in such a way can be terrifying. Raise your foot. No, not that high. Just one fluid motion."

She tried again, her pulse beating wildly, and drove her heel into his foot without pretense. She heard him gasp as he released her. She faced him, curious to see his reaction to what she'd done.

Raynor grimaced and limped a few steps away from her. "That's good. Your natural instinct to protect yourself came through, my lady."

"But I hurt you. I am sorry."

He shrugged. "A small price to pay to know that you learned that particular lesson." He paused. "Let's try one last thing before we're done for the day."

She felt awful that she'd hurt him—but all she wanted was to be caught up in his arms again.

Raynor approached her carefully. "I'm going to place my hands around your throat. Is that all right?"

Beatrice nodded.

His fingers moved to her throat. Instantly, they burned against her skin. She met his gaze, reading the need on his face.

"If someone has you by the throat and they are choking you, you'll faint quickly. If this happens, you must think fast and act accordingly."

Raynor applied pressure to her throat.

"Kick his shins as hard as you can. Grab hold of my arms. That will give you some leverage."

Beatrice held on to his arms.

"When you kick, never use your toes. You might break them and 'twould be hard to run away if you did."

She swung her leg back and then followed through in slow motion, allowing her foot to brush across his kneecap.

"Again," Raynor commanded.

Beatrice repeated the move several times.

"Excellent," he told her, smiling down at her.

Slowly, he began to stroke her throat with his thumbs. Beatrice wanted to melt. Without a conscious thought, she locked her fingers behind his neck and pulled him closer.

At the last minute, his eyes widened as he realized what she meant to do. But it was too late. Beatrice's lips brushed against his.

And the world caught on fire.

CHAPTER FOURTEEN

THE SMELL OF ROSES invaded Raynor's nose as his lips pressed against Beatrice's. He had always thought of himself as a strong man, both physically and mentally. Yet, any resolve he had disappeared when he came near this woman. Everything he knew himself to be changed in an instant.

There was only here—now—with her.

He cradled her face as his tongue ran along the seam of her lips. She opened her mouth to him. As desire burned deep within his belly, he drank in her essence.

Beatrice whimpered. The sound pleased him immensely. His hands moved to the nape of her neck. Her breasts pressed against his chest, causing his manhood to stir.

Raynor broke the kiss. Beatrice gasped for air as his lips glided down her throat and then across to her ear. His teeth teased her earlobe, lightly tugging on it. Her quick intake of breath and low moan brought a smile to his face.

Gradually, he brought his mouth back to hers, wrapping her in his arms, drawing her near. Time stood still as he feasted upon her. Both of their hearts beat rapidly as their bodies touched. His hand cupped her breast, kneading it before dragging a finger across her nipple.

Raynor's heart warred with his mind. It had to stop. This woman belonged to another, no matter how much he wished it could be different. He could go no further. Reluctantly, he dragged his lips from hers, ashamed at how quickly he'd given in to temptation.

But Beatrice was having none of it. Her fingers locked tightly in his hair and she yanked him back to her. Her tongue invaded his mouth. Raynor clutched her. He would enjoy this moment for what it was, drink it in and treasure it always. On those lonely nights when his need for her burned, he would remember these precious kisses.

Because it would be all he had of her—of them—and their time together.

"Enough," he said gently. He took ahold of her arms and eased her away from him.

Beatrice's eyelids could barely stay open. She wore a hungry look, as if she danced on the cusp of satisfaction but had not quite obtained it. More than anything, Raynor wished to be inside her.

Honor prevented him from acting upon his strong desire.

"Raynor." Her voice was ragged, pleading.

"Beatrice," he said softly, still holding her at arm's length. "You must go to your betrothed unspoiled. I have taken far too many liberties with you. We can never do this again."

"Never?" The word echoed in the room. It reverberated in his mind.

"Nay," he told her. "'Tis wrong in so many ways. You are the most beautiful, most desirable woman I have known—but you belong to another. We must end this, here and now. We must never be alone again." He gave voice to the plan he had formed only three days ago, the one he had neglected to follow through with. The plan he must adhere to now.

Tears welled in her eyes. As was her habit, she began nibbling on that full bottom lip. Raynor caught his breath and stopped himself from lowering his mouth to hers once again.

"I will fulfill my duties at Ashcroft. I would ask that you continue to improve matters within the keep during that time. Then, I will see you safely to Brookhaven as I have promised."

Once last time, he cupped her cheek. "But I can no longer be near you in any way, Beatrice. My resolve weakens every time I see you. Smell you. Touch you. Taste you." His thumb brushed gently against her trembling lips. "You have cast a spell upon me, Beatrice Bordel. I fear I shall never find happiness with any woman."

Tears slid down her cheeks. Raynor wanted nothing more than to kiss them away. Silently, her brown eyes begged him to change his mind. Instead, he bent and chastely kissed her forehead. He closed his eyes, savoring the moment. The feel of her. The scent of roses. The smoothness of her skin.

Raynor lifted his head. "I can't speak with you anymore, Beatrice. I don't trust myself around you. There'll be no more lessons or conversations. I will take meals in my room."

His hands dropped to his side. A coldness, deeper than any winter he'd experienced, filled his soul. "I'll let you know when the time comes to escort you to Sir Henry's."

Raynor took her small hand in his. He raised it to his lips and pressed a fervent kiss upon it. "*Adieu*, Beatrice."

He turned away from her. It took all his will to put one foot in front of the other. When he reached the door, he fought the urge to look back at her. Raynor opened the door and hurried down the corridor, heading straight for the chapel.

At this time of day he found it empty, silent as a tomb. Wordlessly, he fell to his knees and then prostrated himself on the floor. Every part of his body called out to return to Beatrice though he knew it was wrong.

Banishing all thoughts of her from his mind, he humbly asked Christ Almighty's forgiveness for having been such a weak sinner and poor knight. He prayed for strength in body and in character. He renewed his vow to serve the king, protect all women, and be an instrument of the Church.

Spent, he rose slowly—determined to stay the course and continue on a path of honor.

BEATRICE SAT IN her chamber, awaiting the meal that Hilda would bring her on a tray. She had tried to eat in the great hall, but sitting by herself was lonely. Raynor never took a meal in her presence. They had only passed each other in the corridor twice in the weeks since he had given up all contact with her. Both times she received a curt nod as he went by, but no words had been spoken between them. She had also caught glimpses of Peter from time to time, but he never acknowledged her presence.

Her rare conversations with anyone had been with Gobert, the steward. Needing coin for goods in order to refurbish the various bedchambers, she'd gone to him on a few occasions.

Beatrice's gaze went to the lute that sat in the corner and she picked it up. She hadn't played the instrument once since the deaths of her loved ones. That seemed so long ago, though only two months had passed.

She'd had a silly fantasy since Raynor began avoiding her. In it, she took her lute down to the great hall to sing and play for the people. Raynor would walk by, drawn to the music. At other times, she fancied that she would be playing the lute in her room late at night. He would stop, listening outside her door. Rapping lightly, she would admit him and sing and play as never before. Her musical skills would capture his heart. He would sweep her into his arms and kiss her as she longed for him to do.

No. 'Twould never happen—thanks to her lies.

The last time they had been together, his kiss had convinced her that she must finally tell him the truth. Explain fully why she had lied. There had been no time to do so. He pushed her away and told her he could no longer be in her company just as she'd been ready to confess her sins and beg for his forgiveness.

And now? Weeks had passed, so it was much too late to share the truth with him now. He might even think that she lied again. If he finally believed that she had no betrothed awaiting her at Brookhaven—even if he could forgive her deceit—she knew they couldn't wed. His brother had expressed an interest in her, wanting to somehow break her imagined betrothal and take her for his wife. In the hierarchy of the nobility, Raynor would be obligated to step aside and allow Peter to lay claim to her. As the eldest son and Baron of Ashcroft, Peter retained all the power.

That was the last thing Beatrice wanted, for it would drive Raynor away from Ashcroft forever.

She learned from Gobert that Raynor had sent a messenger to Brookhaven. Beatrice knew of no reply that had been received and she felt certain the steward would've shared with her if one had come. She wondered how Raynor had worded the missive to Sir Henry and if he mentioned more than escorting her north. Had he referred to her as the betrothed of Edwin Stollers?

Beatrice sank onto the bed, setting her lute aside. She feared after her arrival at Brookhaven, she would be trapped by the lies and then humiliated once the truth came out. Would Sir Henry be willing to help a liar?

More importantly, Raynor would feel so betrayed.

Where would she go?

Bitterness and guilt filled her. A convent would take her in. She could donate the few gold coins she had, sell her lute, and give them her mother's ruby ring. Then she would spend the rest of her life hoping God would forgive her.

Beatrice needed forgiveness. She had killed a man. Nightmares of that night still haunted her. She dreamed of holding the ax in her hands as the robber brutalized her. Each night, she killed him over and over as the flames surrounded them, the screams of the other thief burning to death echoing in the distance.

Beatrice would wake, drenched in sweat and shivering with fear. The images continued to haunt her and they prevented her from falling back to sleep. Because of that, she found herself listless at mass each morning and her appetite had dropped off. Hilda encouraged her to eat each time she brought a meal to her bedchamber, but she only picked at the food.

A knock sounded at the door. Beatrice admitted Hilda, who brimmed with energy.

"My lady, tonight is the harvest home celebration. Would you care to join in?"

"Nay. I need to pack for my journey north. Gobert gave me word today that I leave tomorrow morning."

Hilda set the tray down. "Do you need any help? I'd be happy to stay."

"It's not necessary. I don't have much to gather. Go and enjoy yourself. I want to get as much rest as I can."

"If you're certain." Hilda waited a moment, but Beatrice knew she would not change her mind. She ushered the servant from the bedchamber.

Beatrice knew all about tonight's celebration. The servants talked about it constantly since the reaping had finished and the tying and winnowing had been completed. She heard them describe the food that Cook had prepared, the bonfire being built, and the dancing that would take place. But Beatrice had no reason to attend. She couldn't force any food down and had no one to dance with. And if she did decide to go and saw Raynor dancing with another woman in his arms? It would be the end of her. She refused to ruin the celebration.

A trunk had been sent up earlier in the day, probably Raynor's doing. Since she knew he would insist that she take some of his sisters' old clothes, she sifted through them again. She selected three *cotehardies* of purple, blue, and gold and a few kirtles and smocks. Tomorrow would be a day to wear her own clothing. She bent and touched the hem of her garment to reassure herself that the gold coins sewn into it still remained. Her fingers also went to the pocket that hid her mother's ruby ring.

She hoped Raynor remembered that she would refuse to ride a horse and would have a cart ready for the long journey. Beatrice glanced at the food and left it untouched. Instead, she curled up on the bed and cried herself to sleep.

CHAPTER FIFTEEN

Raynor pulled the currycomb through Fury's coat as he readied the horse for travel. He'd thought long and hard on whether he should venture on this trip with Beatrice but, in the end, she was his responsibility and he would see that she arrived at Brookhaven without any problems.

It puzzled him that no missive had come in return to the one he'd sent to Sir Henry Stollers. As always, he was brief when he wrote since he had no patience for letter making. He'd told the nobleman that Beatrice's mother and grandfather had fallen ill and passed away and that he was charged to deliver her to Brookhaven in time for the wedding.

Despite no response, Raynor knew he could no longer hold her at Ashcroft. The estate was already in good shape. All the wheat had been collected, and he'd put John in charge of the sowing and milling. The women would weave their baskets and spin the wool to make clothing. Raynor had left detailed instructions with Gobert as to what tasks should be accomplished during his trip north. By the time Raynor came south again, hunting and butchering would have started and the meat would be salted, smoked, and stored.

"My lord?" Brice, the young stable boy, stood with his hands hidden behind his back. They'd spent many hours together and enjoyed each other's company. The lad soaked up Raynor's words about how to care for horses and a trust now existed between them. Fury also liked the boy and the horse did not freely show affection to many people.

"Since you're leaving, I brought Fury a treat." Brice pulled an apple from behind his back.

The horse dipped his head. The boy held the apple up to him. Fury made short work of it.

"You'll take good care of the other horses while I'm away?" Raynor asked.

Brice nodded eagerly. "I know what to do. I won't let you down, my lord."

"Good. I'll see you upon my return."

"Will you be gone a long time? As before?"

"Nay." He ruffled the boy's hair. "I intend to return to Ashcroft as soon as possible and plan to stay from now on."

Brice's face lit up. "'Tis good news indeed, my lord." He ran off.

Raynor resumed brushing his horse and, out of habit, began speaking aloud to Fury.

"We've got a journey north, fellow. I'm afraid I'll need to hold you back on the way there, but we'll gallop to your heart's content when we return. Lady Beatrice fears horses, so we must take our time in getting to Brookhaven."

He grew wistful. "I wish I could change how she felt about your kind," he told the horse, unburdening his heart. "I wish I could change many things. Especially when it comes to Beatrice."

"So you love her?" a voice asked.

His brother stood at the entrance to the stall. Not the disheveled version he'd seen when Raynor first arrived at Ashcroft, nor the one who had shaved and dressed in his best clothes when he proclaimed he wanted to marry Beatrice. This version was somewhere in between.

"Truthfully? I do love the lady," Raynor admitted. "I think I have from the beginning." Finally, he'd voiced what had been in his heart—and what he could never tell Beatrice.

Peter leaned against the door. "Tell me."

Continuing to brush Fury, he said, "I doubt she told you much about the night we met. I was riding to Ashcroft from Kinwick and came across an awful scene in the woods. A burning cart. Bodies strewn about. One was her servant that a trio of highwaymen had killed."

"And the others?"

Raynor shook his head, still amazed after all this time. "Lady Beatrice had disposed of two of the robbers, including one who died with an ax buried in his neck. I arrived as she fended off the last thief who attempted to steal her lute."

Peter's eyes widened. "She dispensed with two robbers? She actually killed them? But she's a tiny thing," his brother protested.

Raynor nodded without providing further details. He'd wondered if Beatrice had experienced any regrets.

"At first, I admired her courage and spirit," he continued. "I've grown to appreciate her kindness and intelligence, too. And there's not a more beautiful woman in England." He paused, knowing words would never change the hopeless situation.

"And now you must take her to her betrothed."

The brush froze mid-stroke. "Aye. I promised I would deliver her safely to Brookhaven. We leave today." Raynor put the brush aside. "In fact, it's time to depart."

"You're a good man, Raynor, and have always been a good brother to me. You've cared for Ashcroft and its people when I shirked my responsibilities. I am forever in your debt."

Peter embraced him, and Raynor could not remember the last time that had occurred. He slapped Peter good-naturedly on the back and broke away.

"Godspeed." His brother turned and left him with Fury.

Raynor saddled his horse and then braced himself for seeing Beatrice again.

BEATRICE HAD NOT spotted Raynor at mass that morning. She feared the rift between them had grown so wide that he would charge others with seeing her safely to Brookhaven. Mass ended and she never found him, though he usually stood in the back and slipped away the moment the service ended.

She returned to the great hall to break her fast, wanting to see the grand room one last time. It buzzed with conversations and she assumed most of the discussion centered on last night's harvest celebration. It warmed her heart that Raynor had brought back an Ashcroft tradition. Hilda told her they'd not held one in several years and that everyone had been thrilled to see the old custom revived.

Glancing to her left at the trestle tables filled with soldiers, it was easy to notice the difference in the group from the first time she had laid eyes upon them. The men sat taller than before and their new captain kept a watchful eye upon them. Beatrice could see the physical transformation in many of them, muscles honed by hours of training in the yard. If Ashcroft fell under attack for any reason, these men would successfully protect it from harm—all thanks to their time under Raynor's instruction.

By listening to those around her, she'd gleaned that he also spent part of each day in the fields, supervising the hands involved in the harvest, as well as burying himself in bookkeeping with Gobert. It filled Beatrice with pride to see his efforts recognized and she knew that Ashcroft was in good hands, despite the fact that he couldn't claim to be its baron.

It saddened her that he'd refused to spend time with her during her stay in his home. Beatrice felt it a wasted opportunity. She would have enjoyed Raynor's company even in the spirit of friendship, but she understood why he had broken ties between them. His absence should have prepared her for the day she would no longer see him, but Beatrice only felt the pain of a broken heart.

Lifting her cup, she swallowed the last bit of her ale and stood to leave. As she did, two of the soldiers left their group and came toward her.

A stout one with a blond beard spoke first. "Lady Beatrice, I am Timothy." He indicated his companion. "This is Bobbit. We have been chosen to accompany you to Brookhaven."

"'Twill be a pleasure to see you to your destination, my lady,"

Bobbit added. He had dark eyes that looked as mischievous as a naughty child's might.

Both men had a competent manner about them, but they also seemed friendly, much as everyone she had met during her stay at Ashcroft. She would be comfortable in their company.

"I have a small trunk in my bedchamber that will need to accompany me."

"Lead the way, my lady. We'll retrieve it and secure it in the cart," Timothy said.

Beatrice took them upstairs, pleased to hear about the cart. She shouldn't have doubted Raynor's memory regarding her fear of horses.

They reached her room. She indicated the trunk that was going with them while she claimed her lute.

"You play the lute?" Bobbit asked.

"Aye. I haven't played it for a while, but it's very dear to me. I used to entertain my mother and grandfather with it, but they passed away recently." Beatrice blinked away the tears that formed in her eyes.

"I'm sorry for your loss, my lady," Timothy said. "We are also sorry to see you go. I hope you have enjoyed your stay at Ashcroft. You have certainly transformed the keep."

"It was my small way of trying to repay Sir Raynor."

Bobbit smiled. "He's a good man. I'm sorry he's not the master." He looked around guiltily. "I know I shouldn't be saying so. It's just that Lord Peter's an odd one."

"Sir Raynor truly cares for Ashcroft and its people," Timothy agreed. "As do you, my lady."

Beatrice willed herself not to cry. She despaired leaving the estate behind as she headed to a place that might not embrace her so warmly.

"You'll have to return again and visit someday, my lady," Bobbit said. "Sir Raynor continues to better the place each day. You can come and see all of the new improvements he makes."

"I would like that," she said softly, but Beatrice knew once she passed through the gates of Ashcroft, she would never return.

She led them back downstairs, and they went outside with her trunk. Beatrice turned and saw all the servants from inside the keep lined up, Hilda at one end and Cook at the other. Hugging each of them goodbye, it was easy to thank them for their hard work and friendship. She reminded Hilda of what tasks should be finished next, and then Cook took her aside, handing her a basket.

"I've already given Bobbit some food, but here are a few special treats for you to eat along the way."

"Thank you, Cook. I appreciate your kindness to me." Beatrice hugged the woman again and slipped the basket over her arm.

For the final time, she walked through the doors of the keep and descended the stairs to the bailey. Bobbit sat atop a chestnut horse, next to the cart that awaited her. Timothy rose from the driver's seat and reached out a hand to her.

"If you don't mind, I'd prefer riding in the back so that I may stretch out my legs."

Timothy jumped down. "Of course, my lady." He climbed into the back of the cart and took her lute. Placing it on the blanket next to her trunk, he secured the basket she gave him. Then Timothy handed her up and made sure she was settled, giving her another blanket to drape over her.

Beatrice turned and waved goodbye to those who had gathered to see her off. She kept a smile on her face, though her insides ached with unhappiness because Raynor wasn't there to see her go.

It shouldn't surprise her. After all, he was fulfilling his promise to see that she was escorted to Brookhaven. It didn't mean that he would personally perform the task when he had trusted soldiers that could do so on his behalf. She realized it was too soon for him to leave. He wouldn't want things to fall back into the previous state—yet disappointment covered her more heavily than the wool blanket that sat in her lap.

Beatrice would never see him again. She'd been given no chance to say goodbye.

But she would always remember his kiss.

Timothy flicked the reins and the horse trotted off. As they went through the baileys, Beatrice saw activity everywhere. They passed Donaldus, the carpenter, who gave a shout and jaunty wave to her.

Soldiers on duty appeared on the wall-walk. They, too, waved down at her and she returned the gesture as she looked back at the keep. Though she'd only spent a little over two months living within its walls, Ashcroft seemed more a home to her than the manor house in which she had been brought up. Beatrice brushed a tear aside.

As they approached the gate, she steeled herself for the moment they would drive through it. Her stomach turned as she glanced beyond it and spied Raynor sitting atop Fury.

Waiting for her.

CHAPTER SIXTEEN

THEY HAD BEEN on the road almost a sennight, and each day unfolded much in the same way. Raynor rode ahead of the cart carrying Beatrice and her meager belongings in order to scout the way. Timothy drove the cart, while she watched the passing scenery. Bobbit brought up the rear, keeping his eyes open for anyone that might follow them.

Their party stopped briefly at midday to stretch their limbs and partake in a simple meal before they continued north. By twilight, Raynor would have found a place to make camp.

He hated that time worst of all, being in camp with Beatrice. He always volunteered to hunt for their supper, leaving Timothy and Bobbit to build the fire and gather water. Raynor would return with some small game, cook the meat and listen to the others talk.

The two soldiers spoke of their lives before coming to Ashcroft. Both were fairly new to the barracks, but Raynor had found the two men skilled in the yard during their training sessions. He believed himself a good judge of character and thought each man trustworthy. He had only brought two soldiers with him, thinking Sir Lucas could not spare any more.

More than anything, he avoided meeting Beatrice's eyes as the four of them gathered around the fire for their evening meal. While polite to her and respectful of her station, Raynor observed both soldiers had grown increasingly enamored with her and he couldn't blame them. What man would not be drawn to her?

Beatrice shared small bits of her childhood with them, nothing too specific. She never spoke of her fear of horses, and neither Timothy nor Bobbit asked her about it. Mostly, she listened to their tales—until their third night on the road. Bobbit asked if she would play her lute for them. It surprised Raynor when Beatrice agreed to do so although it took both Timothy and Bobbit urging her on.

Her voice was low and throaty, much as her speaking voice. The words she sang wove a spell as her fingers strummed the strings of the instrument. If he hadn't already been in love with her, Raynor would have toppled deep into the abyss of love after hearing her perform.

From then on, his men begged for her song. She seemed pleased that they did so and obliged them every evening once they had supped. Raynor sometimes could feel her eyes on him as she sang, but he chose to stare off into the distance. Yet, her voice touched his heart each time she sang. Actually, she tore it in two. For as much as he hated being near her as they journeyed north, he lived for each minute in her presence. These were the last precious days he would ever have in her company. Each league they traveled brought her closer to her new life.

Raynor wondered what kind of man Edwin Stollers was. Would her husband care for Beatrice as much as he did? Would he appreciate not only her beauty but enjoy her sweet spirit? Would the nobleman enjoy her intelligence and conversation, and value her kindness and compassion?

He tamped down the jealousy that rose within him, jealousy of a man he'd yet to lay eyes upon and one that he would dislike on first sight. Would he resent this faceless man till the end of time? For 'twould be this nobleman who claimed Beatrice Bordel as his bride. Stollers would give her his name and a home. He would be the man that would take Beatrice to his bed and make sweet love to her. Stollers would be the father of the children she bore.

And in an ironic twist of fate, Raynor would be the fool to deliver Lady Beatrice to the nobleman.

This must stop, he told himself. Misery already filled him. He couldn't imagine what his life would be like once he rode away from

Brookhaven. Raynor pushed aside the gloomy thoughts in order to listen to Beatrice's song and relish the little time he had left with her. If ever there had been a time to live in the moment, it was now.

"What will you sing tonight?" Timothy asked eagerly.

"I want to hear more about Odysseus," Bobbit proclaimed. "I like the man."

"You like hearing about war," Timothy teased, punching his companion in the arm. He looked back to Beatrice. "But what of his home? Odysseus fought for ten years. You've sung tales of war and glory, yet I can't help but think about what Odysseus missed while he was away."

"You are right," she said. "Half a score is a long time to be gone, and it's another ten years before he returns after the fall of Troy."

"Why did it take him so long to make his way home?" Bobbit demanded. "I would think he would be impatient to return."

Beatrice laughed. "Because he had to have many more adventures. Homer let it take Odysseus another decade to arrive back at his starting point so he would have more to write about."

"Well, we arrive at Brookhaven soon," complained Timothy. "We won't have time to hear about all of those adventures. Tell of him coming home, my lady. I want to know he arrived safely and that he had loved ones waiting for him."

She sat her lute aside. "Then instead of song, I shall merely tell you some of his story."

Both soldiers stretched out their legs, getting comfortable as they leaned against a fallen log. Raynor sat atop the log, his elbows resting upon his thighs. He was familiar with *The Odyssey* and knew what Beatrice would share.

"While Odysseus was gone making war and searching for his way back to Ithaca, twenty years had passed," she began. "Most everyone believed him dead. A group known as the Suitors vied for his wife's hand in marriage. Each day they tried their best to persuade her to wed one of them, but Penelope remained loyal to her husband's memory."

"Penelope. I like that name," Bobbit said.

"Hush," Timothy told his friend. "Let Lady Beatrice tell the tale."

Raynor saw her hide a smile before she continued.

"Penelope didn't know it, but Odysseus had already returned. He'd been met by his grown son, Telemachus, who told him about the wicked Suitors and their plans. Together, father and son agreed that the Suitors must be eliminated. That's another story for another night, but Odysseus chose to disguise himself as a beggar upon his arrival in Ithaca. No one knew who he was but the housekeeper, who was sworn to secrecy."

"I can't imagine any servant keeping such a secret," Bobbit remarked.

"But she did," Beatrice revealed, "thanks to the goddess Athena. Athena prevented the servant from speaking to her mistress about what she had learned. Penelope then decided to have the Suitors compete in an archery match, using Odysseus' bow. The one who could string it and shoot through a dozen ax heads would win her hand. She thought it would be impossible for any of them to achieve the feat."

"Of course, Odysseus won," Timothy interrupted. "He would be the only one strong enough and skilled enough to complete the task."

"But would they let a beggar take part in such a competition?" asked Bobbit.

"They did," Beatrice shared, "but Timothy is right. No Suitor came close, and Odysseus won the competition. Along with his son's help, they turned their arrows upon the evil Suitors who wished to usurp him. Every single one was slain."

As she wove the tale, Raynor couldn't help but gaze upon her. He fancied himself as Odysseus and Beatrice as Penelope. He would strike down any man to have her by his side.

She must have sensed his stare, for Beatrice turned and met his gaze. The longing on her face gave away the deep feelings she had for him.

As the two soldiers continued to discuss Odysseus' prowess, Raynor's eyes communicated with hers silently. The strength of their feelings seemed palpable enough to cut through with a sword, yet nothing could come of it.

He mouthed the words, "Can never be," as he shook his head, trying to break the spell between them. Her teeth sank into her lower lip, trying to maintain control.

"It's good that Odysseus returned and that he took his rightful place," Raynor declared to the group. He stood and added another log to their fire. "I will stand the first watch."

THE NEXT EVENING, they approached an inn located in a small village. Raynor went inside and spoke to the innkeeper, finding only one room available. Deciding they would stay there for the night, he told the man to ready it and asked if his men could sleep in the stables with their horses. The innkeeper agreed after Raynor produced extra coin.

He went outside and mounted Fury, doubling back to meet up with his party. They'd passed a few inns along the way and had bought fresh bread at them, but it had been too soon to stop for the day and take advantage of the lodging.

Raynor spurred Fury on, allowing the horse to gallop the remainder of the way. He spied the cart in the distance and slowed as he approached it.

Riding up beside the vehicle, he said, "We are close enough to stay the night at an inn ahead. I spoke to its owner and he assured me that we could reach Brookhaven in another two hours once we set out from there in the morning."

His eyes met Beatrice's. "My lady, it will give you a chance for a bath and a good night's sleep before you meet your new family tomorrow."

She swallowed. "Thank you, my lord. That's quite thoughtful of you."

"My pleasure." Raynor made a decision that he hoped he wouldn't regret and waved Bobbit closer. He wanted some time alone with

Beatrice.

"Since we are so close to Brookhaven, I think it best for you and Timothy to leave in the morning and return to Ashcroft. It won't take you nearly as long riding back. Sir Lucas will be grateful for your swift return. I can hitch Fury to the cart for the last portion of the trip. I plan to stay a few days and make sure Lady Beatrice is settled, then I will return to Ashcroft myself."

"Very good, my lord," Timothy said. He clicked the reins and continued down the road.

They arrived at the inn as the sun set. Raynor instructed the soldiers to take Beatrice's belongings up to the available bedchamber and then told the men to care for the horses.

As they left, he turned to her. "The inn is crowded. Only one bedchamber remained."

She frowned at him. "But where will—"

"I told the innkeeper we are married."

Her eyes widened at this words.

"It's a rough sort that sups in the public room. I believe it's best for them to think you're spoken for and that your husband is by your side. You may sleep in the bed. I'll sleep on the floor in front of the locked door. It never hurts to be too careful in these situations. I simply wanted you to know of my plan before we entered. Will you agree to it?"

Beatrice nodded. "If you think it's for the best, my lord."

"I do," he assured her.

Timothy and Bobbit returned from the stables. Raynor gave them coin for their trip back to Ashcroft and for their meal at the inn. The four entered and immediately a man on the far side of the room shouted, "Bobbit! What brings you here?"

Bobbit went to greet him. He returned and told Timothy that they could dine with his old friend.

"We were pleased to accompany you, Lady Beatrice," Bobbit said. "I hope you visit Ashcroft again one day." He and Timothy gave a bow and went to sit with his friend.

Raynor had asked the innkeeper to prepare a table and food for them. The man indicated where they should sit. Raynor settled Beatrice and then seated himself beside her.

"The fire feels good," she said, holding out her hands.

Raynor sensed that everyone was watching Beatrice. To let these men know she was taken, he reached for her hand and entwined his fingers through hers.

Pleasure rippled through him as it always did when they touched. He squeezed her fingers affectionately and brought their joined hands onto his lap, under the table.

He leaned over. "Remember, you are my wife. We need to let all know."

Beatrice glanced about the room and nodded.

Raynor raised her hand to his lips and kissed her knuckles, his lips lingering on her fingers. She blushed at the contact between them.

"Must you be so brazen?" she whispered to him.

"Every man now knows to keep his hands to himself or he will have me to answer to."

A woman served them cups of ale and then returned with bowls of steaming stew.

They were halfway through their meal when the door to the inn opened. A tall, fair-haired knight entered, taking in the room as he removed his gloves. His gaze stopped on Raynor and Beatrice. Raynor didn't like it. The stranger was old enough to be her father.

The knight spoke briefly to the innkeeper, who handed him a tankard of ale, and then he walked toward their table. All the other tables were occupied.

"May I join you?" the knight asked.

CHAPTER SEVENTEEN

"We would be delighted, my lord," Beatrice said.

The knight sat across from her. She found him quite handsome for his age.

"What brings you this way?" the man asked.

"We come to visit with Sir Henry Stollers at Brookhaven, a few hours north of here," Raynor said.

Raynor's hand tightened around hers. His tone was very formal and she guessed he did not want to reveal too much to a stranger.

"Ah, I know of Sir Henry. And you are?"

"Sir Raynor Le Roux of Ashcroft. The estate lies far south of here. And this is my wife, Beatrice."

Beatrice swallowed hard as Raynor introduced her. She lowered her gaze to the food before her, not wanting to give away their ruse. Then she decided it would look suspicious if she did not engage in conversation with the knight, so she looked up and found him gazing at her thoughtfully.

"I'm happy to meet you. I am Sir Thomas Applegate." He paused as the serving wench brought him his meal. Breaking off a piece of bread, he looked at Beatrice again with interest.

"Forgive me for staring at you, my lady. You strongly favor a woman I knew in my youth." Applegate chewed on the bread thoughtfully. "Are you from these parts?"

"Nay, my lord," she said. "I have lived in the south all of my life."

"And you've never been north. Interesting." He took a sip of the ale and then turned to Raynor. "My lord, where did you foster?"

"In the south, with Sir Lovel. Do you know him?"

"Ah. Lovel. I met him once. He's a fine soldier and a good man."

Beatrice reached for her cup and drank the last of her ale. She liked Sir Thomas' gray eyes and gentle manner, but she found his interest in her a bit disconcerting.

He and Raynor continued to speak, discussing men they knew and places they'd been. Beatrice tried to follow their conversation, but the nearby fire and the stew warming her belly made her yawn.

"I see we are boring your wife," Sir Thomas noted. "May I ask why you have come so far?"

"For a wedding," she answered truthfully. "Sir Henry's grandson Edwin is to be wed soon."

"I doubt his bride could be half as beautiful as you, my lady," Sir Thomas said graciously. He cocked his head and studied her a moment. "I can see you in pearls. They would look lovely against your throat."

Raynor's fingers tightened painfully on hers at this forward remark. She frowned at him and the pressure subsided. But Sir Thomas' mention of pearls caused her eyes to mist over.

"My dear, I'm sorry if I've upset you," the nobleman apologized, picking up on the change in her. "I meant no harm by my words."

"It's quite all right, Sir Thomas," Beatrice said, wiping away a tear with her free hand. "My mother owned a beautiful set of pearls given to her by my father." She smiled at the memory. "Mother said he always told her that they looked lovely against her creamy skin."

"Do you favor her much?" he asked gently.

"Oh, my mother was most beautiful. More so than I ever could be," she shared. "I only wish I had her pearls to remember her by."

"I do not know of these pearls," Raynor said. "What became of them?"

Beatrice turned and gazed up at him. "I didn't mention it to you, my lord. 'Twas after my mother passed," she explained. "I had to use them to settle some outstanding debts."

She bit her lip to keep it from quivering. "I find I am tired," she announced. "It's been a long journey from our home." She looked to her pretend husband. "Mayhap we could go upstairs now?"

"If you'll excuse us," Raynor told their companion. He rose and helped Beatrice from her seat.

"It was nice meeting you, my lord," she said.

"And I will not forget meeting you, Lady Beatrice." He gave her a sympathetic smile. "Good luck to you upon the remainder of your journey. I hope you enjoy the wedding. Give my best to Sir Henry."

Raynor signaled to the innkeeper and led her from the public room. The owner escorted them up a small staircase and down a hallway, then bid them good evening.

They entered the small bedchamber. Beatrice spied her trunk in the corner and her lute perched on top of it. She walked over and brushed her fingers lightly against the strings as she heard Raynor lock the door. She concentrated on the lute, remembering the many times she had played the instrument for her mother. Sweet memories overcame her and Beatrice began to weep.

Raynor came to her and wrapped his strong arms around her from behind. She leaned into the warmth of his chest and drew comfort from the contact that she had sorely missed. His arms snaked about her waist, holding her firmly. She gripped his forearms. He leaned his cheek against the top of her head.

They remained together for some minutes, neither moving. Gradually, her tears subsided. Raynor turned her gently in his arms but kept them about her, making her feel safe. She noticed the frown on his face.

"Tell me again of these pearls, Beatrice."

"Why?"

"Humor me. I want to hear of them and the debts you owed."

She shrugged. "Once Tolly and I buried my mother and grandfather, I went to look through Grandfather's strongbox. My mother had been ill for some time and hadn't worn the pearls in many years. I figured they were safely stored there and I was right." She smoothed her palms against his gypon. "I placed them about my neck, wanting to be close to her again."

Beatrice laid her hands on his chest. "Moments later, Amfrid arrived."

"Who is this Amfrid?"

"He collected the rents in our neighborhood and claimed my grandfather owed him quite a bit of money." She dropped her head. "He . . . he demanded the necklace in payment of the debt."

Raynor's fingers lifted her chin until their eyes met. "And you do not believe this was the case."

"No." The word came out a whisper. Tears filled her eyes again. "I felt so helpless. So alone. I told him . . . I told him . . . that I was betrothed. That once I married, my husband would gladly pay off the debt Grandfather owed. But . . . but Amfrid . . . he told me he would keep the necklace until the debt could be paid in gold. I begged him not to sell it . . ."

Beatrice hated the feelings of helplessness the memory brought. She never wanted to be in that position again and remembered her vow to one day reclaim the necklace.

Her tears flowed freely, knowing the lie had begun that day with Amfrid. She had told *him* she was betrothed. She had continued spreading the falsehood when she met Raynor in the forest days later. Then, she continued the story with Peter at Ashcroft when he expressed interest in wedding her himself. Now here she repeated it again, to the man she loved. Once, Beatrice had wanted to share with Raynor that she was free, but the web of deceit tightened about her like a noose around a condemned man's neck.

Raynor pulled her face into his chest and stroked her back in comfort. Beatrice knew it was the last time he would embrace her in such a tender way. By this time tomorrow, they would be at Brookhaven. Her lies would already be exposed. Raynor, being an honorable man, would never find it in his heart to forgive her for such dishonesty.

Raynor lifted her into his arms and carried her to the bed. Placing her gently upon it, he softly said, "Sleep, my lady," as he stroked her hair.

Beatrice closed her eyes and blocked out the world.

RAYNOR DIDN'T GET much sleep. He didn't want to. Why sleep when he could gaze upon Beatrice?

She had slept through the knock at the door last night. He answered it and found the innkeeper's wife on the other side. She asked when the hot water should be fetched for the lady's bath. He explained how tired his wife was and asked that it be sent up first thing in the morning. The woman looked over his shoulder and saw Beatrice fast asleep. She agreed and said it would be brought upstairs shortly after dawn broke.

He'd returned to the bed, sitting next to Beatrice as he tenderly caressed her cheek while she slept. He held her hand until the candle burned low. Finally, he extinguished it and reluctantly parted from her, retreating across the room. Sitting on the floor with his back resting against the door, he dozed fitfully—until he heard someone moan. He came to, alert and listening for what had awakened him.

Beatrice tossed and turned in bed, whimpering in her sleep. Raynor moved to the side of the bed. She murmured words he could not understand. Her breathing was quick and shallow as if she was in distress.

Her moans turned into a scream. Not wanting the entire inn awakened by the noise, he covered her mouth with his hand.

He held her down as she thrashed about and fought to sit up.

"You're safe," he said over and over. Finally, she stilled, and he released her.

"Was it a bad dream?" he asked quietly as he sat next to her.

"Aye. The nightmares . . . they come . . . every night."

Suddenly, he knew what haunted her. "Do you dream of the highwaymen?" he asked.

"Aye. They chase me. I always search for the ax. I know I need it to protect myself."

He touched her cheek and felt the wetness of her tears. It hurt his soul that she awoke from such nightmares each night.

"You know how to protect yourself, Beatrice," he assured her. "I taught you myself. You took those lessons to heart. Tell yourself as you fall asleep each night that nothing can harm you. Eventually, your body and your mind will believe your words. The bad dreams will end in time."

"I can only hope so."

He heard the doubt in her voice. "Trust me."

He started to stand, but she caught his hand. "Stay. Just a few minutes. At least until I fall asleep again."

"All right." Raynor remained until her breathing evened out. He slipped his hand from hers and returned to his post at the door. But sleep eluded him. Today was the day he would hand the woman he loved over to her betrothed.

After another hour, he heard footsteps mounting the stairs and stood. He unlocked the door and opened it so the innkeeper's wife and her servant could bring the hot water in.

They poured four buckets of steaming water into the tub they'd brought up the previous evening.

"We'll be back with more water and a bath wrap," the servant said, eying him appreciatively.

Raynor moved to the windows and opened the shutters, letting in the dim light. Beatrice stirred, mumbling something.

"I know. It's cold," he said, feeling the brisk breeze enter the room.

She sat up. "It's freezing! Close them."

He laughed. "I'll see that they bring candles. Hot water has already arrived for your bath," he informed her.

The women returned with additional buckets of water and a cake of soap. He asked for more candles, which they brought.

"Do you need help, my lady?" the innkeeper's wife asked.

"Nay, I can manage myself."

After the women left, Raynor turned to Beatrice. "I will leave you to your bath. Come lock the door behind me. I plan to stand guard in the hall and see that no one interrupts you. The innkeeper will deliver our food within the hour."

Beatrice climbed from the bed and walked to the door. "Thank you," she said. "A bath is a special treat after being on the road for so long."

"I know you want to look your best for when we reach Brookhaven."

A shadow crossed her face. He wondered if she worried about what the day would bring.

Raynor stepped into the corridor and Beatrice shut the door. He heard the lock thrown and her footsteps moving away. Leaning against the door, he crossed his arms.

Soon, he heard faint splashing through the door and a soft melody. He closed his eyes and imagined her naked in the tub, singing as she lathered up the soap and glided her hands across her smooth, ivory skin. The thought made him grow hard. He retreated to the other side of the hallway, trying to think of anything else but Beatrice.

Finally, he heard her walking about as the wooden boards on the floor creaked. A few minutes later, Beatrice opened the door. She wore the *cotehardie* she had on when he'd rescued her. Her damp hair tumbled to her waist.

"Do you think we might break our fast downstairs? I would like to dry my hair by the fire."

"As you wish." Raynor offered her his arm.

They descended into the public room and found themselves the only ones there at this early hour. He led her to a table by the fire and signaled the serving wench. She immediately brought ale and bread to their table, giving him a sly smile.

They ate in silence—or rather, he ate. Beatrice simply tore her bread apart and then pulled it into tiny pieces.

"You should eat, my lady. You don't want to grow weak and faint upon our arrival at Brookhaven."

She nodded wordlessly and ate several bites, sipping ale in between. Finally, she pushed it aside and withdrew a comb from her pocket. Raynor could see it was missing several teeth as she began to run it through her hair.

"What's this? Your comb is a sorry sight," he proclaimed.

"Mine was lost in the fire," she told him. "I found this one in your sisters' room."

It appalled Raynor that she was using a broken castoff. He supposed Edwin Stollers would gift her with a jeweled comb. Immediately, the thought angered him.

"Here. Let me help you," he said as she struggled with a snarl in her locks. He took the comb from her and she offered him her back.

Raynor drew the comb through the length of her hair. He forced his fingers to keep from trembling. Finally, he worked out the tangles and had no more excuse to touch her.

"I should return this to you."

She took the comb from him and then ran her fingers through her hair. "I think it's now dry enough for me to braid. I need to return to the room. I left my hair ribbons upstairs."

Raynor nodded and followed her back to their room. He watched in fascination as she arranged and twisted the strands until a single braid fell down her back.

"Are you ready?" he asked.

Beatrice looked up at him, her face devoid of emotion. "Aye."

"I'll collect the cart."

Raynor lifted the trunk to his shoulder and took it to the stables, where he told the departing Timothy and Bobbit farewell. He set the trunk in the cart and attached Fury to the vehicle. The horse looked at him as if he had gone mad.

"I know you've never pulled a cart in your life, but you must for Lady Beatrice's sake," he told the animal. "Now be on your best behavior, Fury. The lady is skittish."

He drove the cart around to the front of the inn. Beatrice awaited him outside, holding her lute. Raynor had already paid what he owed the night before, so they were free to depart.

Beatrice eyed Fury warily. She surprised Raynor when she said, "You may secure my lute in the back. I think I will ride next to you."

Doing as she asked, he lifted her to the bench and came around to climb up next to her. The seat was narrow and their thighs nestled against one another's as he took up the reins.

"To Brookhaven," he said. He popped his wrists and Fury took off at a trot.

Raynor wished the horse would get lost on the way so he could sit next to Beatrice forever.

CHAPTER EIGHTEEN

BEATRICE CLOSED HER EYES for the first few moments of the ride so she wouldn't be able to see the horse. She became accustomed to the rhythm of Fury's hooves clopping along the road. Slowly, she opened her eyes.

The horse truly wasn't as close to the seat as she had thought. Her fear of horses seemed such a small thing now when compared to her fear of losing Raynor, which was much stronger. It was why she chose to ride beside him now. Beatrice needed to be near him for the last hours that they had left together.

Awareness of their legs rubbing against each another as the cart jostled over the road caught her attention. She enjoyed the warmth of his body as their shoulders now brushed. Raynor was a large man and he took up much of the bench seat. Though he made her seem small, Beatrice also felt protected sitting next to him.

As they moved along, she took in the beauty of the early November day. The sun shone brightly, while the cold air smelled crisp and clean. Leaves in an array of colors lined their path.

If only they could continue on this road forever.

Beatrice wondered what would greet them once they arrived at Brookhaven. Her goal was to find a way to get Sir Henry alone and discuss her situation without Raynor overhearing or demanding to be a part of the conversation.

And what of the bride that would be arriving at Brookhaven—was she already there? If not, could Beatrice somehow suppress talk of the wedding until after Raynor left? If she could, he need never know about her lies.

"What were you like as a child?" Beatrice asked, breaking the silence between them.

Raynor's deep laugh was his answer.

"Please tell me."

He eyed her. "I would say I was a most curious boy. That got me into frequent trouble, but my father praised my inquisitiveness. I asked questions of everyone at Ashcroft—Cook and the smithy. The steward. The miller. I would ask about what they did. How and why they did it. I got into everything, everywhere, all the time." He chuckled. "It was probably a relief to my parents when I was sent away to foster."

"I am curious about that practice."

"What?"

"Fostering," Beatrice said. "What is the point of a child leaving behind the very loved ones who could teach him or her? I never went anywhere and learned everything I needed to from my mother and grandfather."

Raynor shrugged. "It's tradition—the way things have always been. I still loved my family, but being raised by another nobleman allowed for him to be more objective in my upbringing. Sir Lovel taught me without favoritism."

"Was it hard being away from home? Weren't you lonely?" she asked.

Raynor smiled. "You would think so, but I thought of it as a grand adventure. My cousin, Geoffrey de Montfort, also was sent to foster with Sir Lovel. We are the same age. We trained together. Went to war together. We are as close as brothers can be."

"Where was your own brother during those years? Did Lord Peter also foster with you at Sir Lovel's estate?"

"Nay. Peter stayed closer to home. He made more frequent trips back to Ashcroft since he would assume the title of baron one day. I know Peter didn't make a good impression on you, but he wasn't always the way he is now."

"I'm glad you had your cousin with you. I assume not everyone is lucky enough to know someone where they foster."

"True. I wish you could have met Geoffrey. And Merryn, his wife." He shook his head, a smile playing about his lips. "You two would get along famously."

"Why?" Beatrice asked, curious about this woman who could cause Raynor to smile.

He glanced at her. A warm feeling grew in the pit of her stomach, then his eyes turned back to the road ahead.

"You both know your minds and are good with others."

She sat a little taller upon hearing him praise her. "I am flattered you think so. You sound as if you know me well when we've only shared a handful of conversations."

This time when he looked at her, she saw the heat in his eyes. "Some people have an instant connection when they meet. I admit that I felt one with you."

Beatrice looked down at her folded hands in her lap, not daring to acknowledge what lay behind his words. "I wouldn't know of this. My life has been an isolated one, with only Mother, Grandfather, and Tolly, for the most part. Grandfather took me to the village on rare occasions, but I never really knew many people. I doubt I would be a good judge of character."

"See? You should have fostered."

They both laughed, then he grew serious. "Are you looking forward to your new life, my lady? You will become mistress of a castle one day. Your children will be born there, and your eldest son will one day assume his rightful place. You will have a history and become a part of the fabric of life at Brookhaven."

Beatrice hesitated. She wanted the life Raynor described.

But she wanted it with him. At Ashcroft.

"Ah, we're here."

She looked up and saw the castle that rose in the distance. The dark, foreboding structure caused her to shiver involuntarily.

"Are you cold? I can fetch a blanket."

Raynor started to reach around to the cart's bed, but Beatrice put a hand upon his arm and stopped him.

"Nay, 'tis not the cold. I am frightened," she admitted.

He would think she spoke of meeting the inhabitants at Brookhaven or possibly a fear of the marriage bed. Instead, her biggest fear was how she would handle losing Raynor's trust. Mayhap she deserved to. Beatrice almost wished her lies would be exposed the moment they arrived. Raynor's rage would quickly drive him away from her. She hoped the anger would remain in his heart so that he could forget her forever.

But Beatrice would never forget Raynor Le Roux—or his kisses. The thought of his touch would stay with her till her dying day.

They continued along the road in silence now, past the empty fields where the harvest had been collected. She grew sick to her stomach as they approached the gate. Raynor stopped the cart and called up to the gatekeeper, giving their names and informing him that they were expected by Sir Henry.

The gates opened and the man on duty gave them directions to the keep. Fury pranced along, taking them through the baileys until they arrived at the stairs leading up to the keep. A thin, balding man met them.

"Welcome to Brookhaven, my lord, my lady. I'll see your trunk is brought inside and that your cart and horse are cared for."

Raynor jumped down and reached his hands out to her. He clasped Beatrice about the waist and lifted her gently to the ground. Turning, he said to the servant, "I must warn you to be careful. Though Fury usually possesses a mild temperament, he is not a cart horse. I'm afraid he will be quite feisty after a morning of pulling us along."

"Very good, my lord," the man said. "I appreciate the warning."

Raynor offered her his arm and they ascended the stairs. Beatrice's heart beat more wildly with each step. She gripped Raynor's arm, glad he steadied her.

The massive door was opened by a tall, lean man. "Greetings. I am

Shem, steward to Sir Henry Stollers. What business do you have at Brookhaven?" His tone was friendly but inquisitive.

"I must admit that I am puzzled," Raynor told him. "I am Sir Raynor Le Roux. I sent a missive weeks ago to Sir Henry, but I never received a reply from him." He indicated Beatrice. "With me is Lady Beatrice Bordel. Unfortunately, her grandfather, a friend of Sir Henry's, recently passed away. I sent word that I was escorting Lady Beatrice to the wedding."

"Ah. The wedding," the steward said, pursing his lips.

"When may we see Sir Henry?" Beatrice asked, eager to speak to the nobleman.

A pensive look crossed the steward's face. He started to speak and stopped.

"Spit it out, man," Raynor said. "We have come a long way."

"Sir Henry and his son are together. 'Tis easier to care for them." Shem gave them a glum look. "I am afraid to tell you that both men are dying."

Shock reverberated through Beatrice.

Dying?

For a moment, she thought this brief reprieve would be welcomed. But if Sir Henry and his son were to pass on, that left only his grandson. She had no link with Edwin Stollers. He would have no reason to keep her on at Brookhaven unless as a companion to his bride. She clung to the waning hope that threatened to disappear.

Beatrice determined to meet Edwin's bride as soon as possible. The noblewoman would also be a stranger here. If they could bond—if Beatrice could convince the woman how valuable she could be to her—she had a chance of finding a home at Brookhaven.

It surprised her when the steward said, "I will take you to them. Follow me."

She looked at Raynor. He gave her an encouraging nod. They followed Shem up the broad staircase. It surprised her that they hadn't seen a servant inside the keep.

They walked down a long hallway, one much longer than the one at Ashcroft. In fact, Brookhaven dwarfed that castle, though Beatrice had thought Ashcroft was enormous. After some minutes, they came to the end of the corridor. Shem opened the door to the solar without knocking and ushered them inside.

Much like Ashcroft, the outer room contained the same type of furniture and would be a retreat for the family in residence. She noted the size and grandeur of everything within it and determined that Sir Henry had done quite well for himself.

Shem said, "Sir Henry fell ill nigh on six weeks ago. One minute he was joking with me, the next, he clawed at his chest and collapsed."

Beatrice's thoughts flashed to her grandfather and how similar the two men's circumstances turned out to be. Dread filled her.

"Sir Guy, his son, has been bedridden for years. He suffers from apoplexy. His right side is paralyzed. He was always frail as both a boy and a man, unlike Sir Henry, who has enjoyed robust health his entire life. But Sir Guy has a fever now. The healer has tried everything, but she said 'twill probably do him in. And Sir Henry grows weaker by the day. It's only a matter of time before they both pass."

"What of the grandson, Edwin Stollers? The one who's getting married," Raynor inquired.

A strange look crossed the steward's face. It seemed to Beatrice that the man wanted to confide something to them but then chose to be discreet.

"Master Edwin fears illness. He is not currently on the Brookhaven grounds. Instead, he's gone to stay at the family's hunting lodge. I'm to send word if either his father or grandfather improves or if one or both dies."

"What kind of man would leave his kin at such a time of crisis? Who's running the estate?" Raynor turned to Beatrice. "Who could wed such a man as this? I have half a mind to return you to the cart and head back to Ashcroft in haste."

She agreed with Raynor. Edwin Stollers' actions were inexcusable.

The steward shrugged. "Master Edwin has never tolerated weakness in others. His mother also died of a fever when he was young. He worried as a boy that he would catch one and do the same. Master Edwin rarely spends time with his father. He has said it is hard to see Sir Guy so helpless and needy, having to be fed and attended to by others. Despite present circumstances, I feel certain he will return in time for the wedding next week. After all, the contracts have been signed."

"Could we see Sir Henry now?" Beatrice asked, trying to take focus away from the upcoming marriage ceremony.

"Aye. I merely wanted to explain the situation to you before you proceeded inside," the steward said. "You'll find Sir Henry through that doorway. I'll wait for you here."

Beatrice moved toward the door and started to knock but thought better of it. She did not want to disturb either man if they happened to be asleep. Instead, she pushed the door open and stepped inside the room.

The bedchamber was twice the size of the one at Ashcroft. A large fire burned in the grate, heating the room, though the chamber still felt chilled. Her eyes fell to the bed closest to the door. In it lay a gaunt man, with thinning, mussed hair and a feverish glow. He was asleep. A woman sat in a chair next to the bed. Beatrice thought that this might be the healer that Shem mentioned.

On the far side of the room, the other bed held an elderly gentleman. Several pillows propped him up in the bed, and she could see he stared at them. He raised a shaking hand and motioned for them to come closer. She glanced at Raynor, who nodded and began to walk the old man's way. Beatrice fell into step beside him.

When they reached the nobleman, she tried to mask the emotions that flooded her. His color was a pale gray, as if he were a fish left to rot in the sun. Watery blue eyes blinked at them in curiosity.

"Who are you?" he rasped.

Chapter Nineteen

"I am Raynor Le Roux, Sir Henry. I was charged with bringing Lady Beatrice Bordel to Brookhaven after her grandfather passed away suddenly."

Sir Henry's face crumpled. For a moment, Beatrice thought the old man might cry. Then he seemed to draw from some inner reserve of strength.

"Henry Bordel was a fine man and an even better friend," he shared. His face softened as he looked up at her. "Come closer, child. Let me see you."

Beatrice came to stand next to the bed. He took her hand and smiled.

"I'm most happy to meet you, my lady. I'm sorry that I am in such poor health as I receive you."

"Your steward said it happened suddenly, my lord."

"Aye. One moment I was full of life. The next? I was felled by a giant pain that tore through my chest, as if a sword had been plunged into me and drawn from my belly to my heart." Sir Henry sniffed. "Overnight, I became weak and helpless."

She squeezed his hand. "The same happened to my grandfather. He went out to hunt in good spirits. Our servant, Tolly, told me that Grandfather felled a stag, the largest either of them had ever seen. As they placed it in the cart to bring it home, Grandfather dropped to his knees. Tolly rushed home with him, but Grandfather was lost to me after we exchanged a few words."

Beatrice wiped away a falling tear, the hurt from that day like an open wound.

"Better that than lingering between life and death. I wonder which breath might be my last." Sir Henry paused. "But I am happy to meet you at last, Lady Beatrice. Your grandfather was so proud of you. You have a look about your eyes of him. He said you had a calm spirit and a giving nature."

She smiled wistfully at what her grandfather had shared about her. "I hope so, my lord."

The nobleman suddenly grimaced. Before she could cry out for help, he went limp against the pillows.

"The pain," he sputtered. "It comes and goes. I'm sorry. I tire easily. Mayhap we can speak more tomorrow."

"I would like that, my lord. We'll leave and let you rest."

Sir Henry held on to her hand a moment longer. "I'm so glad you're here. I want to get to know you, Beatrice, in the little time I have left. And with Henry gone, I hope you'll choose to make your home here at Brookhaven. Now and always."

"Thank you, my lord." Beatrice bent and tenderly brushed her lips against the old man's knuckles.

A heavy burden had been lifted from her. She hadn't had to ask Sir Henry if she could stay. He offered to take her in. She should be thrilled, but as she glanced at Raynor, she noted the puzzled expression on his face.

He took her arm as they moved away from the bed, leading her to a corner of the room. "I find it curious that Sir Henry would offer you a place at Brookhaven. If you are to marry his grandson, would you not live here?"

Beatrice brushed aside his concern. "It's only the ramblings of a dying man, Raynor."

"He did not seem confused to me. Ill, most certainly, but not vague on what went on about him."

"No, but we have only met him."

"I don't care for your future husband, Beatrice," Raynor said, a grim look on his face. "A man shouldn't abandon his family and responsibilities the way Edwin Stollers has. Mayhap he is not the man for you. We should look into breaking your betrothal contract."

She could not believe he thought to attempt this. "And where would I go, Raynor? You know I lost everything I owned in the fire, save my lute. My mother and grandfather are dead. What would you have me do? Go to London and beg on the streets?" Beatrice shook her head. "I will stay at Brookhaven as Sir Henry has suggested. We won't discuss the matter anymore."

Beatrice moved away from him and hurried across the room to the door. Her steps slowed, though, as she saw the healer pulling the bedcovers over Sir Guy. She gave the woman a sympathetic look and crossed into the next room.

"You need to notify Master Edwin that his father has passed," Beatrice told the steward.

RAYNOR AND BEATRICE sat together in the great hall. They had finished breaking their fast. He watched as the serfs and soldiers of Brookhaven filed out of the room, ready to start their day. Servants began to clear dishes from the trestle tables while others pushed the tables back against the wall.

He cursed inwardly, knowing his time with Beatrice drew to a close. All his life, Raynor had wished to find a woman that fascinated him and pushed him to be a better man. He desired one who would stand up to him—and for him. Raynor wanted a lover that he could lavish attention and love upon.

The woman next to him would have been his perfect match in every way—his soulmate—*except for Edwin Stollers.*

"Would you like to try and visit Sir Henry again?" he asked.

"I would. Mayhap we can bring him some comfort in the loss of his son," she said.

They rose in order to go upstairs. At that moment, a stranger entered the great hall. Raynor took an instant dislike to him. He was fair and had wavy blond hair. He looked to be about eight and ten and acted as if he owned Brookhaven. It hit him that Edwin Stollers finally graced them with his presence.

"What have we here?" His voice boomed through the large room. The man sounded arrogant and condescending at the same time. Approaching them, his eyes suggestively took in Beatrice from head-to-toe, appraising her.

Raynor wanted to strike down the young fool.

"Greetings, my lord," Beatrice said.

He smirked. "So you finally arrived. You must be my intended bride. I am Edwin Stollers." He studied her again. "I must say, you are quite fair of face. Much more than I was led to believe. I will enjoy bedding you, my lady." He called out to a passing serving wench. "Ale! Now." He sat at the table they had just vacated. "Come. Sit by me. I would get to know you."

Raynor's anger grew. Edwin Stollers, despite his good breeding, lacked manners. Not only did he treat Beatrice disrespectfully, but the young nobleman ignored him completely. Edwin Stollers was worse than Raynor had imagined he could be.

Beatrice took a few steps in Stollers' direction and then turned, raising her hand back toward Raynor. "My lord, I would like to introduce you to Sir Raynor Le Roux, who was kind enough to escort me to Brookhaven."

"Hmm. I thought your father was supposed to bring you here."

"Do you mean her grandfather?" Raynor decided to join their conversation, invited or not. "She lost him recently—as you have lost your own father. My condolences, my lord."

Stollers flipped a hand carelessly in the air. "My father died long ago. That shell of a man who hovered between life and death upstairs was no father to me." He turned back to Beatrice. In honeyed tones, he said, "But come, my sweet. I want to talk with you."

Raynor watched Beatrice hesitate a moment. She looked from Edwin to him and back again.

Stollers saw what she did and glared at Raynor. "You may go, Le Roux," he said dismissively.

"Where would you have me go?"

Stollers shrugged. "As far as I'm concerned, you've done your duty and delivered my bride to me. Unless," he said thoughtfully, "you're the one designated to hand over her dowry. If her father—or grandfather—made you her guardian. In that case, you can meet with Shem, our steward. He will handle all the financial arrangements. Then you can be on your way. Neither I nor the lady have further need of you."

Beatrice turned pale at the flippant way Stollers spoke. Raynor had no wish to tamp down his fury.

"You, sir, should be more respectful of the lady since she has suffered her loss so recently. I would think that the dowry had been arranged in advance, according to the contracts. Most of all, I hope you'll take the time to acknowledge your own grandfather, who lies dying as we speak, and try to honor your father, who can be buried now that you've finally returned after abandoning him and shirking your duties."

Stollers leapt to his feet. "How dare you speak to me with such insolence!" He glared at Beatrice. "Where did you find such an uncouth escort?" He clasped her upper arm and jerked her close. "I am to be lord of Brookhaven, as soon as my grandfather can put both feet into his grave. I won't be spoken to in such a manner, especially by a retainer of my bride-to-be."

Raynor watched the pain and fear cross her face. "You go too far, my lord," he warned, his voice low and even, as he strode to where the couple stood. Stollers let go of Beatrice's arm and took a step back.

"Who do you think you are?" Stollers cried, his jaw dropping open. "Attacking me in my own home?"

And then the young nobleman began to laugh. "Ah, I see." He glanced from Raynor to Beatrice. "You have feelings for the lady." He cocked his head as he studied Raynor. "Did you know her from the cradle? Pine for her from afar as one of her father's knights? Or did you fall in love with her as you journeyed here, wishing you could run away with her instead of delivering her into my welcoming arms?"

Stollers shook his head. "It doesn't matter. I see on your face what she means to you." He gave Raynor a triumphant smile. "But she's mine, Le Roux. Mine to wed. Mine to bed. I will find joy when I think of how jealous you are every time I dip my wick into her soft folds."

He looked to Beatrice. "My, the lady does look distressed." He brushed a finger down her cheek. "Mayhap you also have feelings for this knight who so gallantly springs to your defense?" He paused. "But you are mine, Minnith. The contracts are signed. We are as good as wed."

"Minnith?" Raynor asked, confused. He looked at Beatrice. "Is this another name you go by, Beatrice?"

He watched her eyes well with tears. "Raynor," she choked out.

"My lord?" Raynor recognized Shem's voice and turned, seeing the steward standing in the doorway.

As Shem made his way toward them, Raynor spied a plain young woman and older man accompanying the servant. My lord. Lady Minnith and Sir Gardeau have arrived."

Stollers made an exasperated sound. "*This* creature is Lady Minnith?" He turned to Beatrice. "By the Christ, woman. Who are *you*?"

THE MOMENT BEATRICE had dreaded arrived in a whirlwind beyond her control.

She stood still as all eyes fell upon her. The young bride-to-be and her father. The steward. Edwin Stollers.

And Raynor.

The ruse had played its course. She found the courage to speak. "I am Lady Beatrice Bordel, granddaughter of Sir Henry Bordel. Sir Henry Stollers invited Grandfather and me to Brookhaven for an extended visit. He looked forward to renewing his friendship with my grandfather and hoped we'd be present in time to attend the marriage of his grandson." She deliberately kept her eyes off Raynor as she spoke.

"So . . . you are not my intended," Edwin said, a thoughtful look upon his face.

"Nay, my lord," she answered. "You assumed as much when you entered the great hall a few moments ago."

Edwin glared at her. "And you did nothing to apprise me of my mistake."

Beatrice wrung her hands. "I did not, my lord."

"Excuse me," Raynor said. He strode from the room without a backward glance.

Her heart cried out for him to stop, but Beatrice remained silent. She turned back to Edwin Stollers.

"I had hoped I could find a place at Brookhaven with my grandfather's passing," she explained. "I am handy with a needle. I also cook and play the lute. When I visited with Sir Henry yesterday, he expressed his wish for me to remain at Brookhaven since I am alone in the world. I hope when you become lord here that you will allow me to stay, as well." Beatrice dropped her gaze to the ground.

"You are far too pretty to cook or clean," Edwin declared. "I would have you remain, though."

She looked up at him. "Thank you, my lord. I am grateful for your hospitality."

"Oh, I wouldn't think of you as a guest," he said, a sly look on his face. "You can serve as my whore."

Both Edwin's bride-to-be and her father gasped. Beatrice froze at the cruel words. She raised her eyes to stare at the man who uttered such filth.

"I'm sure there'll be times my wife is indisposed with her courses. Or her belly swollen with child. I have needs that must be met." He gave Beatrice an evil smile. "You'll do nicely for satisfying those urges, my lady."

"Look here," began Sir Gardeau.

"You'll have no say regarding your daughter, Sir Gardeau," Edwin interrupted. "She will be *my* wife. *My* property. I will do as I see fit since I will rule Brookhaven."

Lady Minnith visibly trembled. She latched on to her father's arm for support. "Father, must I marry him?" she cried.

"No, my child." Gardeau turned back to Edwin. "I wish to terminate the betrothal contract. I won't have my daughter submit to such a coarse man."

Edwin stared boldly at the nobleman. "If you want to break the contract, you will have to pay to do so, good sir."

"Name your price."

Edwin did.

"Done," said Sir Gardeau. "Let us void the contracts. Now."

"Follow me," Edwin said and moved to leave the room. He stopped in front of Minnith. "It's better for both of us that we end our association, my lady," he told the shaking noblewoman. "I fancy Lady Beatrice's looks more than yours. You are too plain by far for me to take you to wife."

Beatrice's temper exploded at his cruel words. "How dare you speak so crudely! You are a rude, insensitive oaf. I hope that no woman ever chooses to wed you."

Edwin marched back to her and dug his fingers into her upper arms. She knew they would be bruised come morning.

"I did this for us," he hissed softly. "I want to wed *you*, Beatrice. I had to do or say whatever was necessary in order to force Gardeau to void the contract. Now stay here like a good girl and let me attend to business."

Before she could reply, his mouth covered hers in a punishing kiss. She tried to pull away, but his hands held her in place. Beatrice did the only thing she could think of.

She bit into his lower lip as hard as she could.

Edwin jerked back. For a moment, Beatrice thought he might slap her. Instead, he smiled. "I like to play rough, Beatrice. I cannot wait to wed you. Have you naked in my bed. I will show you what rough is." He slowly licked the blood along his lip and walked away.

Beatrice watched Edwin Stollers leave the great hall, Sir Gardeau and Shem trailing after him. Lady Minnith gave her a sympathetic look, as if she knew what had passed between them.

More than anything, Beatrice needed to find Raynor—before he left her in the hands of this monster.

CHAPTER TWENTY

RAYNOR PACED THE open space in front of the keep. Anger rolled off him in waves.

Beatrice was not betrothed.

She was free to marry.

Everything he'd longed for could come to pass.

How could he trust a woman who had misled him from the very moment they'd met? One who had continued to deceive him every day and even lied to his brother regarding her availability.

Why would he wish to spend the rest of his life with a woman such as that?

And yet, his heart soared with joy. She wasn't betrothed to that arrogant bastard, Edwin Stollers.

Beatrice could be his.

Raynor thought of her elegant beauty, her compassionate nature, her intelligence, and endless talents. Beatrice Bordel was his ideal woman, the one he wanted to spend a lifetime with. He remembered their shared kisses. Now, he would be the man to introduce her to the ways of love. She would be his in every way imaginable.

Need for her burned within him, overwhelming the anger that had been his first reaction. Beatrice must have had a very good reason for spinning such tales.

He must learn why.

Raynor reentered the keep and went directly to the great hall. It surprised him that only a lone figure stood in the middle of the room—the true bride of Edwin Stollers.

"Lady Minnith?" he called out.

She turned, her arms crossed protectively in front of her.

Raynor went to her. "Where did the others go? Stollers? And Beatrice?" he demanded.

Her mouth trembled. She rubbed her hands up and down her arms, as if trying to ward off something evil.

He realized he needed to gentle his tone. "Are you all right, my lady?"

She nodded. "I will be. Father has gone with that fiend to void the contract. Thank the Blessed Virgin." Minnith made the sign of the cross.

"And Lady Beatrice?"

The young woman's eyes welled with tears. "I feel so sorry for her. To have to wed that man."

"Wed?" Raynor could not believe what he heard. "What do you mean?"

"At first, he told her she could remain at Brookhaven." Her eyes grew large. "As his . . . whore."

Raynor's fists clenched. He held his temper, though, in order to find out what he could from this girl. "What did Beatrice say?" He could only imagine her reaction.

"My father said I could not marry Edwin Stollers and that the betrothal contract must be canceled immediately. The new lord . . . he demanded payment in order to do so. Father agreed. Then Stollers . . . he . . . he grabbed the lady and kissed her, right in front of all of us." She gave him a sorrowful look. "'Twas not a kiss of affection, my lord. He wanted to hurt her. He whispered, but I could hear him. He said . . . awful things to her. She fled, my lord. I don't know where she went."

Raynor gently took her hand and placed a kiss upon it. "I am glad your father discovered Stollers' true nature before you wed him. Excuse me, my lady, but I must find Lady Beatrice."

"Please do," Minnith said. "Get her far away from here. If you don't, I fear for her safety."

Raynor hurried from the room.

BEATRICE KNOCKED UPON the closed door, but no one answered. She opened the latch and entered.

Empty.

She had felt certain that Raynor meant to depart Brookhaven at once, so great was his anger. He might have politely excused himself, but she could see he held back the rage in his taut body. Yet, he hadn't claimed his possessions from his bedchamber. Had he hastened to the stables and ridden out immediately?

Beatrice rushed down the stairs, her skirts held high. She left the keep and ran the entire way, hoping to catch him before he rode away. She pushed past a groom and made it several feet inside the stable before the smell of horses overwhelmed her. She stopped. Terror trickled through her.

She forced it away. Finding Raynor was more important than some petty childhood fear. She lifted her skirts again and continued through the stables. A boy walked by her, but no other person appeared. Beatrice took her time and searched each stall. Finally, she came upon the one holding Fury. The horse nickered to her softly, as if he recognized her. He ambled over and poked his head toward her.

Tentatively, she reached a hand out. With trembling fingers, she stroked the horse's velvety nose. She did it again and then reached up and scratched him between the ears. Fury closed his eyes, a look of contentment on his face. Beatrice grew bolder. She ran a hand under his chin and down his throat. He seemed to enjoy that, so she repeated the action.

Beatrice stepped back, her heart beating furiously. Fury gave a snort of protest and turned away. She let out a long breath.

She had done it. She had touched a horse.

A flood of memories assaulted her. Beatrice remembered being in her father's arms as he held her up to Blaze. She petted the great beast gently, squealing with delight. She recalled the feel of the horse's coat beneath her fingertips. Holding an apple out to Blaze as a treat. Laughing as she sat in her father's lap atop the horse, the world rushing by as they raced along the fence line.

Beatrice dropped to her knees as the memories overwhelmed her. Once, she had loved horses because they had been such a huge part of her father. So many of her recollections of him were tied to horses. And now, she hoped she had conquered some of her fears.

Slowly, she rose, wondering if it was best to wait here for Raynor. He would not leave Brookhaven without his beloved horse.

Then reality banished any hope of Raynor rescuing her from the living nightmare of Edwin Stollers. Raynor was a knight of the realm, faithful to his code of honor. The entire time they had spent together, she had been dishonest with him. No matter what she shared with the knight about Edwin Stollers and the threats he made toward her, Raynor would think she had made her bed and must now lie in it.

She left the stables and returned to the keep, determined to depart immediately. She needed to don her own *cotehardie*, with its gold coins sewn into the hem. Beatrice returned to the bedchamber that held her things. She left on the same kirtle and smock but placed her *cotehardie* over them. Everything else could be abandoned as she made her escape.

Turning to leave, she noticed her lute propped against the wall. Could she make a living as a troubadour? Dare she try to earn a living in this manner? Timothy and Bobbit had liked her songs and stories, as had her family. Beatrice determined anything would be better than staying at Brookhaven. She picked up the lute and left the bedchamber. Her goal was to slip away before Edwin Stollers knew she was missing.

Mayhap she could wait somewhere outside the gates. She doubted Sir Gardeau and Lady Minnith would stay after the debacle in the great hall. They knew of her precarious position. They might even allow her to travel with them if she approached them once they left the estate. Lady Minnith, in particular, had seemed to be kind. It was worth making the effort. If they denied her petition, she would set out on her own.

Beatrice started down the corridor. Before she had traveled the length of two rooms, she heard a voice call out, "My lady!"

The Brookhaven healer hurried toward her. Beatrice remained rooted to the spot, unsure if she should ignore the woman or flee.

"Sir Henry has asked for you," the healer said when she reached Beatrice. When Beatrice hesitated, she added, "He hasn't long in this world, my lady. Father Bernard is with him now. He is performing the last rites."

Though they had only spoken a single time, Beatrice felt an obligation to the nobleman. Knowing the priest had been called upon to perform extreme unction, Sir Henry's time on earth was coming to an end. She would have a brief conversation with him, but she was still determined to leave once it ended.

She followed the healer back to the solar. Her eyes passed over the empty bed where Sir Guy had lain only yesterday. His body had been moved to the chapel to await the return of his son so that a funeral mass could be held. As she approached Sir Henry, she knew the man would soon join his son.

The priest stepped away, allowing her access to the nobleman. Beatrice gazed at the priest.

"You are Lady Beatrice?" he asked.

"I am."

"'Twas kind of you to come, my lady. Sir Henry has made his confession and final prayers have been offered." He paused. "I will wait in the other room. Fetch me when he is in God's hands."

She nodded. The priest vacated the room as Beatrice went to Sir Henry's side.

"You came," he said, his voice weak.

"Aye." She took a seat in the chair next to his bed and placed her lute on the ground beside her. Taking one of his cold, wrinkled hands in hers, she told him, "I am sorry about Sir Guy's death."

"I am, too." He closed his eyes a moment and then opened them again. "It's sad that Brookhaven will pass to my grandson. He's a sorry sort. I have nothing good to say about him."

Beatrice tried to hide her surprise at his words, which were so unlike what he had written to her grandfather.

"I hope . . . his new bride will change him. Mayhap having children will . . . help him mature."

She couldn't tell the old man that the marriage was being called off as they sat here, so she agreed with him. "Aye, my lord. A bride may calm him. And taking responsibility for a great estate such as Brookhaven might be what he needs."

Sir Henry's free hand moved up to rest against his heart. The grimace that flashed across his face let her know he was in great pain.

"I will . . . tell him you . . . must stay." His voice grew weaker. "Mayhap you can become as a . . . sister to him. Be a good . . . influence . . . upon him."

Once again, Beatrice kept silent. She wouldn't disillusion a dying man and tell him she was about to flee the castle because of his conceited, overbearing grandson.

Instead, she thought of a way to soothe him.

"Would you like me to play my lute for you, my lord? I could sing to you of adventure. Tales of glory that would appeal to your knightly nature."

"Nay. Sing of love," he said. "'Tis what matters most. I am at the end of my life. I once knew love." His watery eyes focused on hers. "I hope you will, too, my dear. Mayhap with that young knight you brought. He seems . . . a good man."

Beatrice reached for her lute, too emotional to respond to his words. She let her fingers pick out a melody as she regained control of her emotions. She knew exactly what to sing to bring him pleasure.

Her song was one Odysseus sang to Penelope after all the Suitors had been vanquished. He sang of the twenty years they'd been apart and how he'd longed for her. How he missed not only their life together but also ached by not seeing his son grow to manhood. Odysseus sang of their great love and how it had lasted in his heart across time and space. How happy he was to return and lose himself in

Penelope's arms and in her kiss.

Beatrice finished playing and looked at Sir Henry. She found his eyes closed, a contented smile on his lips. She leaned over and pressed a kiss to his forehead before rising with her lute in hand.

As she turned, she saw Raynor standing a few feet away. She had been so lost in her song that she hadn't noticed his presence.

"I love you," he said, his voice whisper-soft. "I always have. I always will. I don't know why you did what you did or said what you said. It's not important now."

He closed the short distance between them and lifted the lute from her hands. He placed it on the chair and then cupped her face with his calloused hands as his lips touched hers.

The tender kiss told her that, despite everything, all would be right between them.

Beatrice broke the kiss and asked, "Can you forgive me?"

"There is nothing to forgive," Raynor told her.

But she owed him an explanation. "I was so frightened when you came upon me that night in the forest. You were a large, powerful stranger, and I didn't know if I could trust you. I'd already told Amfrid I was betrothed and that my intended would make good on Grandfather's debts. I lied to him because I didn't want him to sell Mother's pearl necklace.

"Telling you I was betrothed seemed a way to protect myself. If you believed I belonged to another man and upheld your knightly code, I would stay safe."

"Knights are honorable. Or should be," he amended.

"I know you refer to Edwin. He is not even old enough to be a knight and should never become one. He is pure evil, Raynor. We must make our way from this place with haste."

He stroked a loving hand through her hair. "We will return to Ashcroft."

"Nay. I can't."

Raynor frowned at her words. "Why not? I want us to wed, Beatrice. I want to spend a lifetime loving you. I won't be complete without you in my life."

She reminded him, "But Peter desires me, too. It would be impossible for us to live there because of that."

"We can go elsewhere," he said, his green eyes intense. "I could be happy in a humble cottage if I lived there with you."

Raynor's mouth came down on hers. Beatrice yielded to him, opening to his kiss. His arms enfolded her, bringing her against his hard chest. She wrapped her own arms around him, stroking his back, happy to think he would finally be hers. Hungrily, his tongue mated with hers in passion, causing her to cling to him as her bones seemed to fade away.

He broke the kiss and told her, "I will love you and honor you all of my days, Beatrice."

Tears sprang to her eyes. "And I shall love you and pledge to be truthful with you always. No matter what."

Raynor kissed her again, a sweet, rich kiss, full of promise for what was to come between them. In that moment, Beatrice knew all would be well.

He released her. "We should leave Sir Henry to rest and make plans to leave Brookhaven at once."

Beatrice glanced back at the bed. Sir Henry slumped against the pillows, his eyes now open and vacant. She leaned over and closed them.

"He's gone," she said. "I need to tell the priest."

CHAPTER TWENTY-ONE

Edwin Stollers insisted Beatrice and Raynor attend the funeral mass that afternoon for Sir Henry and Sir Guy. Raynor had wanted to leave Brookhaven immediately, but he believed in some way Sir Henry reminded Beatrice of her own grandfather. The nobleman had been kind to her. Although it would prolong their stay for a few hours, Raynor knew she wanted to honor their former host by seeing him laid to rest.

They now sat together in the small chapel as Father Bernard chanted in Latin. Raynor took Beatrice's hand. He leaned to her ear and whispered, "All will be well. I promise." He squeezed her hand in reassurance.

Just holding it brought him a peace he had never known. This woman, who had come out of nowhere, had taken over his every waking thought. He looked forward to the life they would build together.

The mass ended. Serfs, servants, and soldiers from Brookhaven began to file out of the chapel.

Raynor said quietly, "We should go to the stables immediately, though it means leaving your lute and clothing behind."

"They can be replaced," Beatrice assured him. "I agree that it's time to depart. I don't trust Edwin Stollers."

"First, I need to find where they placed the cart after we arrived."

"No," she said firmly. "The cart will only slow us down. I'll ride on Fury with you."

Her words shocked him since he knew how frightened she was of horses. "Are you certain?"

Beatrice nodded. "When I looked for you after... after you learned of my deception, I went to the stables. I touched Fury."

"And?" he said encouragingly.

She smiled, her dimple calling out to him. "He was gentle when I stroked him. Petting him brought back childhood memories of my father. We shared a love of horses. I remembered the good times and not the day I lost him. Touching Fury seemed to be my first step in beginning to heal."

Raynor helped her to her feet. They moved toward the door, falling in among those exiting the chapel. "I am relieved to hear this. Not that Stollers has the power to stop us, but horseback will be far quicker than driving a cart. I want to be as far from Brookhaven as soon as possible."

"He is unstable."

"I agree." Raynor knew Stollers had been taken with Beatrice, so much that he had broken his betrothal contract in order to pursue her. Because of that, Raynor planned to marry Beatrice on the way back to Ashcroft at the first opportunity. He wanted to ensure that no man could steal her from him—especially Edwin Stollers.

They blended in with the last of the workers leaving and then turned toward the stables. When they reached Fury's stall, Beatrice greeted the horse. Raynor saw the animal's ears prick up.

"I'll saddle him," he told her. "Stay outside the stall since the space is small." He entered and gave Fury an affectionate pat on the rump.

"Ah, there you are, my lady."

Raynor watched Beatrice turn. He recognized Stollers' voice.

"I wondered where you'd gone off to."

"I came to see Fury." Though her tone was even, Raynor watched the pulse jump in her throat. He knew Stollers scared her even more than horses did.

Fury poked out his head and Beatrice stroked the animal calmly. Pride swelled within him as he saw how she'd begun to conquer her fear.

"My father passed along his love of horses to me," Beatrice said.

"And your lute?" Stollers asked.

"My mother taught me to play when I was young."

The new lord of Brookhaven stepped into view and took hold of Beatrice's arm. "I long to hear you play. Come, my lady." He started to lead her away.

"Stop!" Raynor called out, stepping from the shadows of the stall to join them.

"Le Roux. I wondered where you were." The nobleman glanced inside the stall and frowned. "I hope you weren't leaving so soon. I expect you to attend the banquet tonight in honor of my father and grandfather."

Their host's fingers tightened on Beatrice's arm. Raynor fought the urge to smash his fist into the man's face.

"I found the missives between our grandfathers, my lady," Stollers said easily. "I was touched by their friendship and my grandfather's offer for you to visit us at Brookhaven." He smiled at her. "I'm glad you brought the old man some solace in the end. And I insist that you grace us with your presence tonight since the meal will be in his memory. You can sing and play your lute for us. I know Grandfather would have wanted you there to celebrate his life."

Beatrice looked at Raynor. He nodded his consent because alienating Stollers at this point would be unwise.

"Sir Raynor and I would be happy to attend the banquet, but we must leave first thing tomorrow."

"So soon?" Stollers shrugged. "Then I'll make the most of your company tonight." He pulled on her arm possessively. "Come, my lady. Return with me to the keep. I look forward to hearing you play, for I am very fond of music."

Beatrice glanced back uncertainly in Raynor's direction.

"Go ahead, my lady," he said affably. "I must tend to Fury."

Raynor waited a few minutes since he wanted his next errand to be hidden from Edwin Stollers. He took his time brushing Fury and promised the horse that they would be far from Brookhaven by sunset tomorrow.

Leaving the stables, he returned to the chapel to seek out the priest who'd performed the funeral mass. Raynor hoped the man would agree to his request. As he entered the chapel, a group of men bore the coffins carrying the remains of Sir Henry and Sir Guy past him. Father Bernard walked slowly behind them.

"Father? May I have a word with you before you go to the burial site?"

"What may I do for you, my son?"

"I am Sir Raynor Le Roux of Ashcroft. I escorted Lady Beatrice Bordel to Brookhaven."

The priest nodded. "I've met the lady. And I saw you enter Sir Henry's bedchamber shortly before his death this morning."

"I have something important to ask of you before we return south tomorrow. We wish to be married before we set out on our journey."

Father Bernard gave him a knowing look. "I suppose this might have something to do with the young lord voiding his betrothal contract this morning."

Raynor decided silence was best in this case.

The man shrugged. "You'd be surprised what a priest hears. What he sees when no one is looking. What others tell him even beyond the confessional."

"Then I'll be blunt, Father. I fear for Lady Beatrice. I am sworn to protect her." He paused. "And that includes keeping her safe from men such as Lord Edwin Stollers."

"Do you love her?" the priest asked.

Raynor couldn't hide his smile. "I do love her, Father, with all my heart. I would move mountains for her if she asked me to do so."

"Then I have some advice for you, Sir Raynor. Remember that it's the small things that touch a woman's heart. Pick wildflowers for her when she least expects it. Massage her sore feet when her belly is swollen with your child. Talk with her—not at her. And never take her for granted."

The man of God paused before continuing his counsel. "Most

important of all, tell her you love her each day. Show your love, for all to see. Though many believe it turns a man weak, they are wrong. Love strengthens a man."

"I can say that I'm a better man for knowing her, Father. I will take your words to heart."

"Then I'll be happy to bless your union. When do you wish to take your vows?"

"We've been invited to stay for tonight's feast in honor of the old lord. Could we meet you at midnight? We plan to leave Brookhaven at first light."

"I'll wait for you outside the chapel, my son," Father Bernard assured him. A twinkle came into his eyes. "And I can provide two discreet witnesses to your union."

Raynor took the priest's hand and grasped it in friendship. "Thank you, Father."

BEATRICE CHANGED INTO a blue *cotehardie* trimmed with gold piping. Tomorrow, she would wear the one with her hidden coins when they left to return home.

Home.

Would they make Ashcroft their home? She'd already voiced her concerns to Raynor if they did so. She didn't want to hurt Peter Le Roux by flaunting their love in front of him, but she wouldn't be comfortable living there as Raynor's wife if his brother grew bitter. Raynor had spoken of a small cottage, but Beatrice wondered if he could be happy in such a place since he'd lived in grand castles his entire life.

The important thing was to make their way from Brookhaven as soon as possible. She didn't like the idea of them staying another night with Edwin Stollers as lord. Beatrice thought it in poor taste to hold a feast on the very day both his father and grandfather were buried. She assumed Edwin did so simply because he could. No mention had been made of any other siblings, so she supposed he inherited everything with the deaths of the two men.

Beatrice hoped she and Raynor could leave before the castle's occupants awoke. It worried her that Edwin had many soldiers at his disposal. She guessed that Raynor agreed for them to stay another night so that Edwin wasn't offended or upset. Now that the young nobleman held the title, he could prove to be a powerful foe.

Hoping to quell her nerves, she combed her hair out. Grandfather enjoyed combing her hair when she was young, and the motion had always soothed her. It made her wish that she could have gotten to know Sir Henry better since he reminded her so much of her own grandfather. At least she had brought the nobleman some small comfort in the end with her song.

Beatrice braided her hair again and reached for her lute. With the instrument in hand, it was time to make her way to the great hall.

A knock sounded at her door. She answered it and found Raynor standing there, looking handsome and confident. It thrilled her that this dashing knight with the mesmerizing green eyes had forgiven her transgressions and actually professed his love for her. She had to be the luckiest woman in all of England.

He stole a quick kiss from her. "I long for more, sweetheart, but we are due downstairs." His eyes sparkled as he promised her, "There will plenty more of those to come."

Raynor offered her his arm and took the lute in his free hand. Beatrice felt his warmth radiating beneath her fingers and squeezed his arm.

They reached the great hall, which was almost full. Shem, the steward, met them.

"My lord awaits you on the dais. I'm to escort you to him."

"My friends," Edwin welcomed them as they approached, his arms held wide. "Come and join me for our feast. We have boar and partridge. Eel and salmon. Heron and swan. A meal fit for a king."

The new Baron of Brookhaven seated Beatrice on his right and had Raynor sit to his left. She hated being separated from Raynor but kept her dissatisfaction to herself. Edwin indicated they'd share a trencher.

She took a sip of wine from the goblet before her.

Course after course arrived, but she only picked at the food. A somber air hung over the room. She guessed the inhabitants of Brookhaven weren't pleased with their new lord's decision to treat tonight as a celebration when they should have been in mourning.

The last course finally came. She forced a few bites of it down before Edwin rose to his feet.

"Good people of Brookhaven," he addressed them, a broad smile on his face. "I know you held Sir Henry and Sir Guy in great esteem. It's the reason why I wanted us to celebrate their lives tonight."

Lifting his wine glass, everyone present followed suit. Holding the cup high, he said, "I hope one day to be as wise as my grandfather as I rule over Brookhaven with a lovely lady by my side."

Beatrice felt a multitude of eyes fall upon her. Her pulse beat wildly. She feared Edwin might announce their upcoming nuptials and then they would truly have a serious situation to contend with.

But the moment passed. Instead, he spoke of how hard everyone worked at the estate and how valuable their contributions were in keeping the property running smoothly. She began to relax.

"And finally, I have a treat from the special lady seated next to me." He glanced down and gave her a smile. "Lady Beatrice Bordel has agreed to entertain us with her lute. So pour more wine for us all and enjoy the music."

Nerves rushed through Beatrice at the attention she now received. Her mouth grew dry. She took a long sip of wine and swished it around before swallowing it. Retrieving the lute Raynor had placed in the chair beside her, she slipped it into her lap.

Taking a calming breath, she decided to play a few of the songs she'd sung on the road that Timothy and Bobbit had seemed to enjoy. Beatrice started with the secret inside the Trojan horse and the surprise attack that occurred after the unexpected gift was rolled inside the city gates.

After each song, hearty applause filled the great hall, soothing her nerves. Her voice grew weary, so she decided to end with something different.

"I'd like to share a last song with you," she told her audience. "It's the very one I sang to Sir Henry before he passed on. He didn't ask for songs of glory and adventure. He told me he'd known love and thought it was what mattered most. This is what I played for him."

The large room quieted as Beatrice plucked the strings again. She began the familiar song of Odysseus and Penelope, though this time her heart sang it for Raynor. With every line that Odysseus proclaimed his love for his wife, Beatrice expressed her tender feelings for the gallant knight who had come to be her entire world.

When the last note sounded, no one moved. Beatrice thought she'd done something wrong before the thunderous applause began. Cheers called out her name and that of Sir Henry's.

Beatrice finally found the courage to look across at Raynor. She hadn't been able to glance at him during the song because of the strong emotions that filled her.

His warm smile told her he'd received her message and was pleased with how she'd played.

"You exceeded my expectations, my lady. Thank you for making tonight such a blessed occasion," Edwin said.

She'd become so lost in her song and her love for Raynor that she'd forgotten Edwin Stollers sat nearby.

"I'm very tired after my performance, my lord. I hope you'll excuse me from the remainder of the festivities."

"Of course, Lady Beatrice. I'll see you tomorrow."

Raynor spoke up. "Let me escort you to your chamber, my lady." He stood and removed the lute from her lap and then offered his hand to help her down from the dais.

It took several minutes to make their way through the great hall. Many people came up and told her how moved they were by her song. Beatrice listened as they shared how Sir Henry would have been both proud and delighted by her performance. A few even mentioned in hushed tones that she'd honored Sir Henry in an appropriate manner.

Finally, she and Raynor escaped and made their way upstairs.

When they reached her bedchamber, Raynor lifted her hand from his arm. He turned it over and placed a searing kiss in her palm, causing her heart to skip a beat.

"Do not undress tonight, Beatrice," he instructed her.

His words puzzled her. "Why not?"

He grasped her elbows in his hands. "I've arranged for Father Bernard to marry us at midnight. Rest, for I know today's events have tired you. I'll return for you so we can slip away and meet the priest at the chapel door."

Happiness filled her. Beatrice pulled Raynor's face to hers and kissed him with enthusiasm.

He finally broke the kiss. "I thought it best," he explained, "to be wed before we begin traveling south. I wanted to make sure you're mine." Raynor kissed her tenderly. "Don't mention our actions to Stollers if we see him in the morning."

He pressed a chaste kiss upon her forehead. "I'll return for you shortly."

Beatrice entered the chamber, butterflies dancing in her stomach. Tonight, she would be wed. That would include Raynor loving her, making her his—in every way.

CHAPTER TWENTY-TWO

"Beatrice. Wake up, love."

She opened her eyes and found Raynor beside her bed. The candle burned low.

She sat up. "I didn't think I would fall asleep."

He cupped her face tenderly. "It was a trying day. I doubt you've ever had such an eventful day, sweetheart."

"But you forgot the best part," she said. "When you forgave me for deceiving you. When you told me that you loved me."

"Oh, that?" he said, his eyes dancing with mischief.

Beatrice punched him playfully in the arm.

Raynor rubbed where she had hit him. "You may be small, but you're most strong, my lady. I suppose I'll have to watch what I say in the coming years."

"Remember, my lord, you are the one who taught me how to defend myself." She arched her eyebrows. "The next time you displease me? I might go for your nose. Or worse."

He traced her lips with a finger. "I hope I'll never displease you, Beatrice. I plan to tell you every day how very much I love you."

His lips brushed against hers, and their warmth spread a pleasant tingling throughout her body.

Raynor broke the kiss and pulled her to her feet. "Come. We must hurry. I've checked the great hall and everyone has bedded down. We need to watch, though, for anyone that may roam the halls."

They quietly exited her bedchamber and found the dimly lit corridor empty. Luck was with them. They passed no one as they left the keep and crossed the inner bailey to the chapel. Beatrice made out three figures lurking in the shadows at its door. One had to be Father Bernard. As they drew closer, she recognized Shem, the steward, and the healer she had spoken to earlier.

The priest greeted them. "These two will serve as witnesses to your union."

Both gave them friendly smiles. Beatrice knew they risked Edwin Stollers' wrath with their presence tonight. If he learned of their participation, she could only guess at what their punishment might be.

Father Bernard spoke briefly of the sacrament of marriage, then he had them repeat their vows. Raynor's voice was strong and sure as he gazed into her eyes. Beatrice repeated the identical words, binding her to this knight for all time.

The priest asked if Raynor had a ring to give his bride.

"Nay, Father. I didn't know when I left Ashcroft that I would be marrying the love of my life." He gave her an apologetic yet tender look. "But I plan to purchase one as we journey home. I will have it blessed."

Before the priest could continue with the ceremony, Beatrice spoke up. "Wait, Father." She pulled out the ruby ring from her pocket and held it up.

"This ring was my mother's wedding ring, a gift from my father. If you would bless it, 'twould be a symbol of our love for one another and a daily reminder of the brief happiness my parents experienced."

She handed the ring to Father Bernard for his blessing. The priest did so and then passed it to Raynor. He slipped it on her finger, repeating after the priest his intentions to love and honor her always.

"You are now joined in holy matrimony in the eyes of God and those of man," the priest intoned. He nodded to Raynor. "You may now kiss your bride, my lord."

Raynor needed no further urging. He drew her to him and gave her the slowest, sweetest kiss she'd received from him. Beatrice marveled that she was now this loving man's wife. She swore to herself that not only would she honor, respect, and love him till her dying day but also protect him from all harm.

"Usually, we'd go into the chapel for mass at this point," Father Bernard said, "but given the late hour, I believe we should return to our beds. Have no worries. You are married."

"I can't thank you enough, Father, or our two witnesses, for honoring my request to see that we were wed before we leave for Ashcroft." Raynor looked at the healer and steward. "I hope we haven't endangered you. Know that you have our gratitude."

"Sir Henry would have been pleased with your marriage," Shem said. "It's worth the risk we take. We also know things will change at Brookhaven with his passing—and not for the better."

"I wish I could offer you each a place at Ashcroft," Raynor replied, "but I'm not at liberty to do so. My older brother is its baron."

"No worries, my lord," the healer said, "but if you ever find a need, send for us. Shem and I would be happy to come south and make our home elsewhere."

Father Bernard excused himself and went inside the chapel. The others walked back to the keep and silently entered. They tiptoed past the great hall. Beatrice and Raynor gave a wave and turned to ascend the stairs.

Raynor led her back to her room. He followed her inside and locked the door. A single candle burned in the bedchamber. Beatrice looked up at her new husband and found Raynor drinking her in. She shivered in anticipation of what would come next.

He took her hands in his and threaded their fingers together. "You have nothing to fear, love."

"I'm not afraid," she replied. "Nervous? Somewhat. But I trust you."

"Did . . . did your lady mother tell you anything of the marriage bed?"

"Nay. Her last years were spent in poor health. She did not speak much. Frankly, I never gave marriage a thought. I think Grandfather may have been considering a match for me before he died, but I'll never know." She smiled. "I do know that he would've approved of you, Raynor. You're everything that Grandfather respected in a man."

"I hope so." He led her to the bed. "Remember, what passes between a man and woman is sacred. I will cherish you always, Beatrice. I hope to make you happy."

She gazed up at him, her heart bursting with love. "You already have."

He gave her a deep kiss. Beatrice couldn't imagine being happier than in this moment, sharing a kiss with her new husband.

Raynor stroked her face tenderly. "We may be legally wed, but we must consummate our marriage to make it official. To do that, I need to rid you of all these layers of clothing."

He removed her *cotehardie* and then lifted her kirtle and smock from her, gazing down at her in wonder.

"By the Christ, Beatrice, you are lovely. I am in awe of your beauty." His hands cupped her breasts as he gave her a lingering kiss.

As his fingers kneaded her, a pulsing ache began inside. Beatrice gripped his waist. He broke the kiss and trailed his tongue down the slender column of her throat, all the way to her bare belly, bringing new sensations that she longed to explore. Then he knelt and removed her shoes and hose.

She now stood unclothed before him.

Raynor swept her into his arms and placed her gently on the bed. He quickly stripped off his own clothing. Beatrice stared in awe as he stood before her, naked in the flickering candlelight. His shoulders looked even broader than before. A mat of hair on his broad, muscular chest ran down to a flat belly and beyond. His manhood now stood at attention. She swallowed, surprised by the size of it and having no idea what came next.

"Are you pleased at what you see?" he asked.

Overcome with emotion, Beatrice only nodded.

"Rise from the bed," he said. "I want to turn back the bedclothes."

She scrambled off. Together, they eased the covers back and slipped into the bed. Raynor drew the sheet over them and then faced her as they both lay on their sides.

"May I loosen your braid?" he asked. "I would love to see your hair unbound."

Lifting the long braid, she watched as he undid the ribbon that anchored it in place. Slowly, he parted the pieces, unraveling them until her hair fell to her waist. His fingers ran from her scalp to the ends, over and over. She stretched sensually, satisfied by his touch.

Then he nuzzled her neck and ear, his breath warm against her skin. The ache within her turned into a throb. The throbbing began a primordial beat within her. It built as his hands caressed her breasts, then the curve of her hip, and skimmed along her thighs. Slowly, he parted her legs and touched her at their apex. She gasped in shock as he thrust a finger inside and began stroking her slowly, instant pleasure radiating within her.

"Oh. My." Her breathing began to quicken.

Little flutters danced in her stomach. The throbbing beat stronger and harder as another finger entered her and he moved it more quickly. He kissed her again, his tongue imitating the movement of his fingers. Beatrice found it hard to breathe. Her hands went to his shoulders, her nails digging into his skin. His kiss grew more demanding as his hand worked its magic.

Then a quivering began deep inside her. It built until a sudden explosion of sensations erupted and spread through her, warm as sunshine. Beatrice arched her back as Raynor's mouth moved to her throat, nipping in tiny love bites as his fingers kept up their steady motion. She dug her nails deeper into his back as wave after wave of pleasure rippled through her. She cried out, but his mouth quickly covered hers, silencing the noise as she rode the undulating wave through the storm of pleasure.

Exhausted, her hands fell from his shoulders. She lay limply on the bed as he hovered over her. Their eyes met.

"What I do, I must do quickly," he whispered.

Before she could reply, he removed his fingers from her and replaced them with his manhood. With one push, all the beauty of the moment vanished. Once again, Raynor's mouth kept her from making a sound. He continued to kiss her but held still within her.

Beatrice felt the driving need begin to build within her again.

"'Twill never hurt in the future, my love," he assured her. "I had to break through your maidenhead, but now you will only find pleasure in what we do."

She could feel him pulsating within her. Slowly, he began to move, in and out.

He was right. The brief moment of pain had vanished, replaced by a hunger she'd never known. Each thrust filled her. She clung to him, drawing him deeper. The rocking became faster, harder, more intense. Once more, Beatrice held on for dear life.

The pleasure intensified, even greater than before. As it peaked, she sensed something within him did, as well. Their mouths joined as their bodies had and she felt as if they truly became one.

Spent, he collapsed upon her. She welcomed the feel of him, before he rolled to his side. Raynor stroked her face.

"I love you," she said.

"And I love you." He brought his arms about her and cradled her tenderly. Her last waking thought was how much she loved this bold, daring knight.

Raynor awoke, a feeling of contentment immediately filling him. He looked down at the amazing woman nestled within his arms. She stirred slightly as he brought her closer. He kissed the top of her head and returned his head to the pillow.

What a night they had spent. The first time they'd made love, he was mindful of her virginity. He knew he had pleasured her. Twice more during the night they had joined, each time more satisfying than the one before. Though he had few worldly goods, Raynor was rich in love for this exquisite creature.

Running a hand through her dark brown locks, he fingered the silky strand at the end. Only married for a few hours, love already burst from him. Was it possible to love Beatrice more than he did at this moment? Then he thought to the time when his babe would fill her belly. As the years went by and she gave him sons and daughters, Raynor knew his heart would swell with the love that would grow each day between them.

Raynor brought a hand to her breast and teased the nipple with his thumb. Beatrice moaned softly. Slowly, her eyes fluttered open. She turned and gazed up at him sleepily.

"Good morning, Wife," he said. The use of the word brought him immense satisfaction. His thumb grazed her nipple again and she shuddered, another moan slipping from her lips.

Beatrice reached for his cheek and brushed her fingers across it. "Good morning, Husband," she murmured, her voice low and throaty.

Just the sound of her voice and the feel of her in his arms made him want her again. Hot desire flooded him. He pressed his lips to her temple while his fingers skimmed down, splaying across her bare belly, hoping his seed already grew within her.

Then he remembered the gift he had for her. Slipping from the bed despite her protests, he found where he'd left his clothes and pulled the blue garter from his pocket.

Bringing it back to the bed, he smiled and slid the blue band over her foot, past her trim ankle, and up her shapely calf to rest above her knee.

Beatrice eyed it with curiosity. "What is this?"

"It's a garter, my love, a very special one. It came from Geoffrey and Merryn's wedding many years ago." His hand stroked her bare leg. "I've always kept it with me. I waited all this time to give it to the woman who stole my heart. It's a symbol of my affection and faithfulness."

"Then I plan to wear it always." She broke out in a brilliant smile. "And I'll give it to our oldest daughter on her wedding day."

He drew her close and kissed her passionately.

A harsh knock sounded at the door. Raynor's hand immediately flew to Beatrice's mouth to silence the gasp she uttered.

"It's locked," he whispered. "Go. Speak through the door but allow no servant inside."

He lifted the bedclothes back and watched her walk to the door.

As she reached it, another knock sounded. "Lady Beatrice! Are you there?"

She swung around to face him, a look of alarm on her face. Edwin Stollers stood on the other side of that door.

"Answer him," mouthed Raynor.

"I'm sorry, my lord. I was asleep. Your knock woke me," she called out. She placed her hands against the door, pushing against it as if she tried to keep Stollers out.

"I thought I'd escort you to morning mass."

"I . . . I am not even dressed, my lord. I . . . I must have been exhausted to still be asleep."

"Then I'll return after mass and take you to the great hall to break your fast. I must speak with you on a most important matter."

"All right. I'll see you then."

Raynor had not realized how late the hour grew. He'd wanted to be dressed and gone from Brookhaven by this point. Now they would need to make an appearance before they left.

Beatrice hurried back to the bed and climbed in. She curled against him, her body trembling in fear.

"What if he knows?"

He lifted her chin till their eyes met. "He couldn't. And even if he did, it's done. He might covet you, sweetheart, but Edwin Stollers will never possess you."

She buried her face against his bare chest. "He frightens me, Raynor."

He allowed her to stay within the safety of his arms for a few minutes before he pulled away.

"I must return to my chamber. You need to dress and be prepared for when he returns. I'll see you downstairs." He gave her a swift kiss and rose from the bed.

Beatrice pushed back the covers and stood. Then he watched her gaze fall to the bed. She gasped.

"It's only blood, dearest. It came from when I pushed through your maidenhead."

"But what if he sees it?" she said, panic sounding in her voice.

"He won't. But if he did, merely tell him it was the start of your monthly courses."

Her mouth fell open. "You know of such things?" she asked.

Raynor laughed. "I had two sisters. Two very talkative sisters. It was hard not to hear their complaints when they reached womanhood. They rued the day they were not born men."

She chuckled. "I can't imagine having that conversation where a brother could hear."

He put his arms around her. "I hope you will hear many of those conversations between brothers and sisters, for I wish us to have five sons and five daughters. No, make it six sons and four daughters."

Beatrice laughed aloud. "It's my fondest wish to have many children, Raynor. I hated being an only child. I spent so much time alone."

He gave her a kiss. "You'll never be alone again, love. You'll always have me." Though he wanted to stay and make love to her again, they couldn't waste any more time. He dressed hurriedly and she did the same.

"I'll meet you in the great hall. Bring only your lute. We'll depart after we break our fast."

Raynor opened the door and cast a glance back at the woman who'd changed his life. He stepped into the corridor and shut the door behind him. As he turned, a soldier blocked his way. The man slammed a quarterstaff into Raynor's midsection. He doubled over, the breath knocked from him. Then someone struck his head with great force. Raynor fell to his knees as the world went dark.

CHAPTER TWENTY-THREE

COLD WATER HIT RAYNOR square in the face and he leapt to his feet. Immediately, a chill enfolded him. He'd felt that same chill before—when he'd gone to the dungeon at Kinwick and found Geoffrey de Montfort locked inside a cell.

Someone stood before him, on the other side of the iron bars between them.

Edwin Stollers.

Raynor took two steps forward and grasped the bars that imprisoned him in the tiny space. He kept silent, waiting to hear what kind of game the nobleman played.

Stollers looked amused. "What? No questions? Are you all brawn and no brains, Le Roux?"

He ignored the taunts, not rising to the bait the nobleman dangled. Though Raynor would love to shout at the bastard to burn in Hell, the new Baron of Brookhaven had the upper hand at the moment.

"I'm sorry you didn't appreciate my hospitality. I know you planned to depart today, but I'd prefer you remain my guest for a while. Below stairs." Stollers smiled. "I'll care for Lady Beatrice above stairs, however."

Raynor's grip tightened on the bars. This brash fool would have his guts spilled soon enough. He exercised patience as he glared at his captor.

"You know, I voided my betrothal contract with that plain cow that arrived yesterday because I was so taken with Lady Beatrice. The lady is beautiful beyond compare, so I plan to wed her." He laughed.

"I'll be the envy of every man who sets foot inside Brookhaven. And I have you to thank for delivering her to my doorstep, Le Roux. Why, even Grandfather would have approved of Beatrice as my bride, not only because of her gentle breeding, but for her sweet nature. At times, she's a little too spirited for my tastes—but like a wild stallion, I'll break her."

The young nobleman took a step toward the bars. "I've already enjoyed a kiss with her, and I look forward to tasting her. Every part of her."

Raynor finally spoke. "Then why keep me here, my lord? I've brought her to Brookhaven as I pledged to do. I was to see her safe and settled. It's time I return to Ashcroft, my family home, since my brother hasn't been well. At this time of year, I need to supervise the slaughtering of game and winterizing the cottages on our estate."

Stollers frowned in confusion. "I thought you were leaving today with the lady in tow."

Raynor must be careful. He walked a fine line now and Stollers had all the power.

"Lady Beatrice came to Brookhaven at Sir Henry's invitation. With his death, she believes she has no place here. I agreed to take her back to Ashcroft with me for the time being since she requested I do so."

"But would you choose to marry her once you arrived? Give her a home?" Stollers asked. "What of your feelings for the lady? You seemed . . . upset . . . when you found out she was not betrothed to me."

"I'll admit I was taken in by her looks and charm, but Lady Beatrice has lied to me repeatedly. I wouldn't choose a deceitful wife if I were so inclined to marry. Besides, I'm a second son with no fine home to offer her. You have that and a title. Why would any woman choose me over you?" Raynor shrugged. "Women want stability and protection. Both can be had if they marry a man such as you. As mistress of Brookhaven, Lady Beatrice would have instant wealth and respect. I can provide neither of those to her."

Raynor pressed on. "Release me so that I may journey home, my lord, and meet my family obligations. I'll go alone. Lady Beatrice is welcome to stay and become your wife if you choose."

The words tasted like dust in his mouth, but he saw Stollers contemplate them carefully.

"You'll remain here for now, Le Roux. Mayhap after I wed the lady, I will grant you your freedom." Stollers turned abruptly and hurried away. Two soldiers stepped from the shadows and accompanied him.

Despair flooded Raynor. How could he keep that monster away from Beatrice when he was imprisoned—and no one knew where he was?

A KNOCK SOUNDED on the door, gentler than the harsh rap that had come only an hour before. Beatrice took in a large breath and expelled it slowly as she walked to answer it.

She opened the door and found a smiling Edwin Stollers, dressed in a rich burgundy color. The young nobleman looked confident and in a very good mood.

"Greetings, my lord."

"And the same to you. I hope you received enough rest, my lady."

"Thank you, I did. Yesterday proved a long day for me with too much excitement. I've lived a quiet life in the country and I'm not used to so much activity."

She joined him in the corridor and he offered her his arm. Beatrice reluctantly took it, not wanting to touch any part of him.

"Life in a large castle does not appeal to you?" he asked, leading her away from the bedchamber.

She knew his question tested her, so she thoughtfully replied, "I couldn't say. I only know what I've experienced at the manor house with my mother and grandfather. The three of us and a single servant lived together since my father and grandmother passed on long ago."

Beatrice suddenly realized they'd turned in the opposite direction of the staircase and tamped down her rising panic.

"Where are we going, my lord? I thought we were to go to the great hall to break our fast."

"We do go to break our fast," Stollers said smoothly. "I simply wanted a more private setting in which to do so."

"But Sir Raynor will be waiting for me," she said, worried what Raynor would do if she didn't appear soon.

"Sir Raynor can wait a bit longer. Come." He placed his hand over hers and guided her to the solar at the end of the hallway.

Leading her inside it, Beatrice saw a serving wench remove a final item from a tray she held. Food and drink sat on the table for them.

"Anything else, my lord?" the girl asked.

"No. Leave us."

His sharp tone caused the servant to hurry from the room. Once the door closed behind her, Beatrice felt isolated and frightened.

"Have a seat." Edwin indicated the bench beside the table.

Beatrice did as he requested. She had no appetite, but she and Raynor would be traveling for most of the day. She needed to try to eat something.

"May I offer you some cheese?"

"Please."

As he cut her a few slices from the round, she pulled off a small piece of bread from the loaf and chewed on it. He laid the cheese in front of her and then poured cups of ale for them. She drank some but found it hard to swallow. Stollers had taken a seat beside her, much too close for comfort. His thigh brushed along hers. Beatrice wanted to scoot away, but his leg rested on the folds of her skirt, pinning her next to him.

"I asked you here for a special reason, Lady Beatrice. That's why I wanted time alone with you."

She nervously tore at the bread in her hands.

"You know I sent Lady Minnith away yesterday."

Beatrice's temper flared at the mention of his rude behavior to the young noblewoman.

"I believe you disapproved of my actions?"

"'Tis not for me to judge you, my lord," she said meekly.

"Please, call me Edwin."

Beatrice lifted the cup to her lips, trying to hide her disgust.

"I didn't think we would suit," he continued, his finger lazily circling the rim of his pewter cup.

"The matter is between you, Lady Minnith, and her father," she said as she set her own cup down.

His hand shot out. Strong fingers locked around her wrist. "The minute I saw you—when I thought *you* were my bride—I knew I was blessed with a woman of great beauty and poise."

"But I was not your intended," she pointed out.

"Yet, I wanted you to be." His thumb stroked the tender underside of her wrist, bringing a wave of nausea to her. "Sweet Beatrice, I was smitten from the moment I saw you. I could have no other. Only you. That's why I ridded myself of Lady Minnith. My heart told me I had to be free to wed you."

"My lord—"

"Edwin," he uttered, his fingers tightening on her wrist.

"Edwin." She found the word foul on her tongue but kept an even tone so she wouldn't betray her feelings. "I am no one. I would bring you no dowry, for I am penniless." She waved her free hand about, emphasizing her point.

He grew still, an odd look upon his face. His eyes focused on her left hand.

The one which wore the ruby wedding ring.

She hadn't taken it off since Raynor had slipped it onto her finger last night.

"Not quite penniless," he noted. "That's a fine ring you wear. I haven't seen it on your hand before."

Beatrice thought quickly. "This ring belonged to my mother. I wear it every now and then to feel closer to her." She swallowed. "I told you that Mother taught me to play the lute. When I returned to my bedchamber last night, I was happy from the compliments I received after I played for your people. I took the ring out and put it on. Somehow, I feel my mother's spirit with me when I wear it."

He nodded in approval. She was glad he seemed satisfied with her response.

He lifted her hand to his lips and kissed it. "I will take you with only your lute and ruby ring as dowry, but I *will* have you as my wife, Beatrice. As a woman alone in the world, you lack protection. Sir Raynor pointed that out to me. He said women long for security and protection. He even told me since I had a great estate and a title, it would be what *you* would desire."

She started in surprise. "Raynor said that? When did you speak of this?" she demanded.

"Just a bit ago."

Cold fear formed in the pit of her belly. "I thought you left to attend mass," she said. Her voice shook, betraying her terror.

He wrapped both his hands around one of hers. "Nay. I decided a conversation with Le Roux would be a better use of my time."

Her thoughts raced. Had he seen Raynor leaving her room?

Where was Raynor now?

"The knight in question pointed out to me that as a second son, he had no home to give you. No wealth to shower upon you." Stollers gave her a triumphant smile. "I have both and I place them at your feet."

Her brows knit together. "I am most flattered, my lord."

"Edwin."

"Edwin," she choked out. "But . . . might I speak with Sir Raynor?"

His eyes narrowed. "You seek his approval to marry me?"

Beatrice was speechless. Her mind went blank. Fear began to swallow her.

"So quiet, little mouse?" he teased. "It seems so unlike you. Here, have more ale."

He released the grip on her hand and refilled the pewter cup. She downed it, her mind spinning.

"You may visit Le Roux later. Once I have my answer."

"Answer?" she asked weakly, knowing exactly what he meant.

"To my offer of marriage," he said evenly. "In fact, I'll accompany you to the dungeon. Together, we can share our good news with him."

Fear now paralyzed her. She wanted to flee the room, but her limbs felt heavy. "Raynor is in . . . your dungeon?"

"He is. I wanted to make sure he held no undue influence over you. You alone need to make your decision to wed me. Without his input."

A firm rap sounded at the door.

"Come!" Stollers called out impatiently.

Shem, the steward who had witnessed her marriage vows, entered. If he was surprised to see her alone in the solar with the master of Brookhaven, he hid it well.

"My lord, a rider has arrived from Ashcroft. He says he has a missive for Sir Raynor. I can't seem to locate him."

"Bring this messenger to me at once."

"Very good, my lord." The steward exited the solar.

"You aren't to utter a single word," Edwin commanded. "I wouldn't want a careless word from you to inflict any . . . pain . . . on Le Roux."

The threat hung in the air. Beatrice felt faint. She gripped the bench with both hands, willing herself not to black out.

The nobleman rose and began pacing the solar. He left her to her thoughts till Shem arrived again, this time bringing the man from Ashcroft with him.

She recognized the soldier from seeing him at meals in the great hall, but she couldn't remember his name in the fog clouding her brain.

He stepped forward and saw her. "Lady Beatrice. 'Tis a pleasure to see you again."

She dipped her head in acknowledgement.

"I came across Timothy and Bobbit on the road as they returned to Ashcroft and I made my way here. They were full of praise for your songs that made the journey north most pleasant."

Beatrice smiled and nodded again. She hoped the man would stop addressing her. She didn't want to do anything to endanger Raynor.

The soldier turned to Stollers. "My lord, I have a missive for Sir Raynor Le Roux from his brother, Lord Peter. He's to read it at once and return to Ashcroft in haste."

Stollers reached for the parchment. "I'll see that he receives it. Sir Raynor is in the forest hunting with some of my men at the moment. They seek a boar in order to provide meat for my wedding feast." He looked across to Beatrice and gave her a fond smile. "The lady and I will wed tomorrow."

The rider broke out in a wide smile. "Then congratulations are in order, my lord. I hope you have a long and happy union." He handed over the scroll.

"See that you stop in the kitchen and receive some refreshment before you leave," Stollers said, his manner and tone friendly. "And have Cook give you some meat and bread to see you on your return trip."

"Thank you, my lord." He bowed and looked to her again. "I hope you find every happiness at Brookhaven, my lady."

Beatrice beamed at him as if she were the happiest woman in all of England.

The Ashcroft man excused himself and vacated the solar.

"You did well," Stollers said. He took a seat across from her and broke the seal on the missive. Unrolling the parchment, he said, "Let's see what message is so important."

He squinted and began to read. Beatrice watched him scan the page before him, then he roared in laughter.

Stollers lifted his eyes to hers. "It seems Lord Peter Le Roux has renounced his claim upon Ashcroft. The nobleman has left to enter a monastery. And the title of baron and all the land that comes with it now belong to his younger brother—Sir Raynor Le Roux."

CHAPTER TWENTY-FOUR

R*AYNOR WAS NOW Baron of Ashcroft?*
Beatrice wanted to shout to the heavens. Raynor would be the perfect lord for the estate. He cared for its people and had a fine eye for detail. The land would thrive under his leadership.

And she would be Baroness of Ashcroft and could continue the work she'd started when she briefly resided there. She would be able to renew the friendships she's started and form new ones. They would raise their family within the castle's walls. Why, she might start riding again now that her fear of horses had dissipated. She visualized lifting a small child and seating him atop a pony, leading him around the paddock as Raynor cheered the boy on.

But none of this could come to pass if they didn't escape Brookhaven. Beatrice might have the help of the trio present at her wedding to aid her getaway, but how were they to free her husband? It might be best to leave Raynor behind and go for help.

But where would she ride?

Though they'd passed many places close to Brookhaven, she drew a blank. And if she didn't flee soon, she feared finding herself standing before Father Bernard again, with Edwin Stollers as the designated bridegroom. Beatrice could predict his erupting anger when she refused to speak any vows. 'Twould be even worse when she revealed to him that she was already a married woman—and that the marriage had been consummated under his roof.

Without a doubt, Stollers would see Raynor dead upon hearing that news. Beatrice could imagine the arrogant nobleman rushing down to the dungeons and killing her husband.

A life without Raynor would be no life at all. Beatrice needed him by her side as much as she needed the very air she took in.

A knock startled her from her thoughts.

"Come." Stollers pushed aside the scroll in front of him.

Once again, Shem entered the solar. His gaze avoided her as he looked to his master.

"The messenger from Ashcroft is being cared for in the kitchen. Have you need of me for anything else, my lord?"

Stollers rose. "Aye, find Father Bernard. I need him at once."

The steward's eyes flicked briefly to Beatrice and back to Stollers. Beatrice held her breath.

"He's not here, my lord." Shem did not elaborate.

An annoyed look crossed Stollers' face. "Where the Devil did he go?" he demanded.

Shem shrugged. "Father Bernard left after the funeral mass for your father and grandfather because the bishop sent for him. The priest should return in three or four days' time."

Beatrice knew Shem lied—to protect her.

"Why wasn't I informed of this unexpected trip?"

Shem had the grace to look puzzled. "Sir Henry never asked for the priest to do so, my lord. Father Bernard is required to meet with the bishop twice a year. He was past due on their appointment but put it off since Sir Henry was in such poor health. He wanted to be here to conduct his funeral mass." Shem swallowed and continued. "And your wedding, my lord. Father wished to be present to preside at your vows. Of course, that will not happen now with Lady Minnith gone."

"But I have a new bride that has replaced her." Stollers glanced over at her. "Lady Beatrice has agreed to marry me. We'll wed immediately once Father Bernard returns. Notify the guard at the gatehouse that the priest is to be brought to me upon his return, whether it's day or night."

"I see." Shem grew thoughtful. "Then we should make full preparations." He acknowledged Beatrice for the first time. "Mayhap my lady would like to meet with Cook to help plan your wedding feast? And I know the castle seamstress would be more than happy to discuss a bridal gown with you."

Shem held out a hand as if to usher her to the door. "If you'll follow me, my lady, I can take you—"

"No," Stollers interrupted. "That's not necessary. Cook can do as she pleases. She knows of my favorite dishes. Whatever she decides for the feast will suit me well."

"But Lady Beatrice—"

"She will like what I like and eat what's put in front of her. You're dismissed."

The steward inclined his head. "Very well, my lord." He glanced to Beatrice and gave her a brief nod, an apologetic look in his eyes as he departed.

Beatrice felt trapped. Would Edwin not even let her out of his sight until Father Bernard supposedly returned from his visit with the bishop? And what if Edwin learned of Shem's deception in the meantime from someone else?

She rose from the bench, conscious of the blue garter about her leg. She moved toward the door to see if Stollers would stop her from returning to her room. Beatrice reached for the door handle.

Before she could turn it, she was jerked back. Strong arms encircled her, pinning her own to her side.

"You aren't going anywhere, my lady," Stollers whispered into her ear. "Though the marriage vows may have to wait a few days, I plan to have you in my bed. Now. Your bare flesh against mine."

His thumb and forefinger grazed her nipple and then pinched it, twisting it painfully. Beatrice gasped in shock and outrage. She squirmed, trying to escape his hold on her.

Stollers chuckled as she struggled against him. He drew his tongue along the nape of her neck. "I can't wait to bite into your tender flesh, Beatrice." He squeezed one of her breasts. "I think I'll start with this plump one."

She drew her foot up as she had practiced with Raynor and

slammed her heel down onto his foot as hard as she could. Stollers yelped like a puppy that had been kicked and released her.

She needed to incapacitate him. She swung around and punched him hard in his throat. Immediately, his hands went up and clutched it as he choked.

Stollers turned a murderous eye upon her. "Bitch," he spit out.

Her foot had already drawn back and sailed toward him. She realized that he knew what was coming but couldn't act fast enough to prevent contact. Beatrice kicked his groin with everything she had. Stollers cried out pitifully and doubled over. It still wasn't enough. The bastard would be determined to chase her down once he recovered. Using what her husband had taught her to do, she slammed into his nose with her forehead. Blood spurted as he cursed at her. He bent again, one hand cradling his broken nose and the other his bruised manhood.

Beatrice shoved the nobleman away. As he fell back, he struck his head against the corner of the table. He collapsed on the floor and didn't move.

A flash of the dead highwaymen surrounding her cart in the forest brought her to a standstill. Her body began to tremble as she worried she might have killed the nobleman. Beatrice forced herself to push that thought aside. She must be strong for Raynor. Reaching her husband was what was important now.

Still, she knelt beside Stollers' body and held her fingers under his nose. A warm bit of air tickled them. Relief swept through her, knowing he was still alive.

Beatrice hurried to the door and left the chamber. She didn't care who saw her as she ran down the corridor to the staircase. At the bottom, she saw Shem passing and called out to him. He paused, surprise flitting across his face as he hurried to meet her.

"I struck Lord Edwin," she said as she sucked in quick, short breaths of air.

"You must flee, Lady Beatrice, while you can," the steward warned.

"I can't leave without my husband," she said. "Show me where the dungeons are."

He shook his head. "I've already checked. Sir Raynor is being guarded by three men. We won't be able to free him."

"I won't leave without him."

"You must," Shem told her. "I promise I won't let him be hurt."

Beatrice bit her lip, trying to hold back the tears. "But Stollers will be so angry. He would kill Raynor to spite me."

"I won't allow it," the steward assured her once more. "I can convince him that Sir Raynor is his bargaining tool, something to lure you back. I'll make him understand that you must see Sir Raynor alive and well."

Beatrice knew time was short and that what Shem said was true.

"Quickly!" he hissed, taking her elbow and leading her outside the keep. He rushed her along to the stables.

"Where's his horse?" Shem asked when they arrived.

Beatrice led him to Fury's stall. The steward went in and saddled the beast for her to ride. Though she thought she'd conquered her fear when she stroked Fury's nose, could she ride the large horse? Alone?

She didn't know if she could do it.

As Shem finished readying the horse, Beatrice moved to Fury. She touched him gently and whispered, "I have need of you, Fury. Raynor depends on us. I'm putting my trust in you. You must take me away from here so we can bring help."

The horse nickered back to her, as if reassuring her they were a team. She dropped a kiss onto his nose and gave him a final pat.

"Are you ready, my lady?"

Beatrice nodded and allowed Shem to help her into the saddle. She offered a prayer to the Virgin Mary to watch over her as the steward led her from the stall and out of the stable.

Once they cleared the structure, he gave her a quick nod and hurried away. She turned Fury and rode to the gate, her heart pounding the entire way.

Slowing the horse, Beatrice called up to the gatekeeper. "Did the rider from Ashcroft already leave Brookhaven?"

"He did a few minutes ago, my lady."

"Then open the gates. I have a missive that he neglected to retrieve upon his departure. It's important that it make its way back with him."

The gates swung open without question. Beatrice dug in her heels and Fury took off. They raced down the road, past the harvested land she'd seen only a few days before. As the horse galloped, she began to feel as one with him. Relief, then exhilaration, filled her as they rushed down the open lane.

Within a few minutes, she spied the Ashcroft soldier up ahead. She would ride till she reached him—and hoped he would know where to turn for aid.

Beatrice shouted as she closed in on the rider. She waved frantically. He turned his horse and stopped in the middle of the road to wait for her.

"My lady?" he said as she brought Fury to a halt next to his horse. "What's wrong? Why are you riding Sir Raynor's horse?"

She took a moment to catch her breath. He patiently waited until she could speak.

"Please remind me of your name," she asked.

"I am Ronald, my lady."

Beatrice nodded at him. "Ronald, Sir Raynor is in trouble and needs our help."

"Did he fall during the hunt?" Ronald's brow creased with concern. "Or does something else ail him?"

"Raynor is being held in the dungeon at Brookhaven. He was not out hunting as Edwin Stollers would have you believe. And I am Sir Raynor's wife. We were married late last night and planned to leave for Ashcroft a few hours ago." She paused. "Until we were detained by the baron."

Ronald rubbed his chin. "So you're not marrying Lord Edwin? Why would he lie about this? And why imprison my Lord Raynor? For he is Baron of Ashcroft now, my lady. This was the news I brought in the missive." He thought a moment. "That makes you our baroness."

"I already know of this, Ronald. Lord Edwin broke the seal and read the missive. He wishes to marry me."

"But if you are already married—"

"He doesn't know this yet," Beatrice shared. "I fear if he did, he would have Raynor killed and make me a widow, eligible to marry him."

Ronald looked perplexed. "Then how are you here? We must go back and fetch Lord Raynor before harm comes to him."

"I escaped Brookhaven by striking Lord Edwin. Guards watch my husband, so I wasn't able to set him free. I rode after you, Ronald, hoping you'd know what to do."

He sighed. "I'm a good soldier, my lady. I take orders and am well trained with sword and pike alike. I would take an arrow for you or my lord. Die for you if I must." He shook his head in sorrow. "But I'm only one man. It will take many more to rescue Lord Raynor."

"Then we must ride in haste," she urged him. "We're much too close to Brookhaven and the soldiers that can be sent to hunt me down. We must find a place of safety and figure out what to do."

Beatrice spurred Fury on. Ronald fell in behind her. They had ridden a good two leagues to the south when she saw a group of men approaching from the opposite direction on horseback. She slowed her horse and Ronald did the same.

As he pulled alongside her, she said, "Let's see who these men are and if they can help free Raynor."

She tugged on Fury's reins and allowed the horse to trot toward the men. As they came closer, she recognized Sir Thomas Applegate among them. Before she could call out a greeting to him, a man broke away from the pack and hurried toward them. Beatrice got an odd feeling. Somehow, this rider looked familiar to her.

He brought his horse next to hers and said, "By the Christ! After all this time. It's really you, Beatrice. You are the image of your mother."

CHAPTER TWENTY-FIVE

HIS WORDS SHOOK HER to her core. Beatrice studied the handsome stranger's face, which didn't seem strange at all. Somewhere, from long ago, she had once known this man.

And loved him.

"Who are you?" she asked, studying his dark hair and brown eyes, fighting to remember him from her past.

He leapt from his horse and crossed to her. Beatrice found his hands about her waist, pulling her to the ground. The man engulfed her in his arms and murmured, "Thank God Almighty and the Blessed Virgin. We have finally found you."

Beatrice watched as Ronald dismounted, his hand resting on the hilt of his sword. The soldier didn't draw it, though, as this man didn't seem to be a threat to her.

The stranger pulled away, resting his hands on her shoulders. Beatrice noticed tears staining his cheek, even as he smiled at her.

"You don't remember me?" he asked gently.

She bit her lip in thought. "I feel I knew you once. Long ago. Your voice sounds familiar to me. I also know your smile."

"I am your uncle, Beatrice. Gilbert Lovet. I am your father's younger brother."

Her hands flew to her mouth. The dreams of her father came to mind. In them, he strongly resembled the man standing before her. Then memories exploded within her. She pictured this man tickling her. Swinging her. Placing her on his shoulders. She saw her father chasing them, her uncle swearing she was his as he ran away. Beatrice giggled atop him, one hand threaded in his hair and the other waving at her father.

"Uncle?" she said softly, shaking her head in wonder.

"Aye, Beatrice. Uncle Gilbert." He embraced her again and kissed her cheek. "I thought I might never see you again."

"I . . . I . . . didn't know . . . that I had . . . family. Mother never mentioned you."

Gilbert's large hands stroked her hair. "Lucy was very distraught when Richard died. Do you know, for a moment, I thought you were her? You look exactly as she did at your age."

"Oh, Mother was most beautiful. I am not."

Her uncle laughed. "Of course, you are. You're a Lovet. We are known for our good looks."

"But . . . I am Beatrice Bordel."

He frowned. "Bordel was your mother's maiden name. She was the daughter of Sir Henry Bordel. I suppose she chose to raise you under that name."

Beatrice slowly nodded. "Aye, Sir Henry Bordel was my grandfather."

Gilbert put an arm about her shoulder. "Your mother suffered after she lost your father—it weakened her mind. It made her withdraw. She rarely spoke. And then one day, she was gone from Lovet Castle. We didn't know where to find you."

"We lived with my grandfather in his manor house," she said.

Her uncle looked at her steadily. "I can't understand why your mother slipped away and hid you from us all these years, but I assure you that you *are* a Lovet. I'm afraid Lucy's sorrow may have turned her against us." Gilbert took her hands. "Believe me, Beatrice, when I tell you that we looked high and low for you. You had another grandfather and grandmother that were heartbroken at the loss of their son—and you. I inherited the title and estate upon my father's death since Richard was gone. And in all these years, I've never stopped looking for you."

Gilbert looked to Sir Thomas, who'd left his mount and came to stand next to them.

"Thomas is my closest friend. He knows how hard I've tried to locate you."

"And then I met you by pure luck at that tavern, in the company of your husband," Sir Thomas said. "I recognized you straight away. You are Lucy made over. When I heard your name was Beatrice, I knew I must ride in haste to tell Gilbert. I had no doubt that his niece had been found. It was why I seemed so curious as to your final destination and asked so many questions. I apologize if I seemed rude."

Her uncle smoothed her hair. "You have family to meet, Beatrice. Though your grandfather passed away several years ago, your grandmother is still alive. Then there's my wife and our four children—your cousins. We'd be honored to have you come to visit us. It would give us a chance to become acquainted with you again."

Beatrice's head swirled with all of this news. To think she had family. It bewildered her that her mother had left her husband's kin behind without a word. It also hurt to know that she'd grown up alone and isolated when she could've been surrounded by all her cousins at her father's home. She couldn't let these thoughts overwhelm her, though, for she'd found the perfect people to help bring Raynor back to her.

Beatrice would rely on her family.

"I'm truly pleased to meet you, Uncle." She glanced to Sir Thomas. "And I thank you, Sir Thomas, for your role in this reunion. But I must ask something of you and the knights that accompany you."

"Ask anything, child," Gilbert said.

"My husband, Lord Raynor Le Roux, Baron of Ashcroft, is being held in the dungeons at Brookhaven. We need to rescue him from the madman that placed him there."

She quickly explained how Edwin Stollers had become enamored with her, glossing over the fact that he'd voided his own betrothal contract to marry her. Beatrice also kept secret that she and Raynor had been married for less than a day. Sir Thomas had met them when they pretended to be husband and wife, and she would leave him with that impression. They only needed to know that Stollers was obsessed with her and had imprisoned Raynor so he could marry her.

"This is very troubling," Gilbert said. "To think a nobleman would act in such a despicable manner."

"He is nothing like Sir Henry Stollers, his grandfather. He is barely a man, drunk on his new title and power since Sir Henry's recent death. We must rescue Raynor. I can't live without him. He is everything to me."

"Never fear, Beatrice." Gilbert strode toward his men. Sir Thomas followed him.

Ronald turned to her. "You have a formidable uncle, my lady. The Lovet name is well known, even in the south. You couldn't have found a more powerful ally."

Beatrice expelled a long sigh of relief. She offered thanks to the Blessed Virgin for watching over her and bringing her uncle and his men to her in such a time of crisis.

Ronald handed her up onto Fury. She clasped the reins firmly as her uncle and Sir Thomas also mounted their horses.

"We ride for Brookhaven!" Gilbert called.

His horse darted forward to lead his men, with Sir Thomas bringing up the rear. Beatrice and Ronald fell into place behind them. The quick pace her uncle set had them back at the gates of Brookhaven in no time.

"Gatekeeper!" roared her uncle.

Gilbert Lovet was no longer the sweet, affectionate man who'd spoken softly to her upon their meeting. Beatrice now saw the warrior coming out in him. This was a man who would let nothing stand in their way. Raynor was as good as freed.

"My lord?" the gatekeeper called, his eyes skimming over the group that numbered a dozen men with her uncle.

"The Earl of Lovet wishes to see the lord in charge of Brookhaven. Open the gates now," he commanded.

Beatrice hadn't known Uncle Gilbert was an earl. She realized he was far more powerful than Edwin Stollers, in both title and riches.

His good character, too, was obvious. Stollers would never be the man her uncle was.

She grinned. Raynor was going to love her new family.

They rode through the gates and crossed the outer and inner baileys at a brisk pace. Gilbert brought their horses directly to the steps of the keep. He and Sir Thomas dismounted while his ten knights remained in the saddle. Ronald helped her from Fury's back, and the four of them climbed the stairs and entered the keep unannounced.

"I left Stollers in his solar," Beatrice explained. Before she could continue, the quiet inside the keep was broken with a single word shouted for all to hear.

"Whore!"

She glanced up and saw Stollers racing down the stairs, madness in his eyes. His swollen nose dominated his face. Dried blood remained on his chin and ran down the front of his *cotehardie*.

Before she could react, he reached her, his fist raised to strike. Gilbert stepped between them.

"Do you know who I am?" her uncle asked, his voice low and deadly.

Stollers blinked several times and stepped back, as if he only now saw that others stood with her. "I . . . do. My lord, what brings you to Brookhaven?"

Gilbert took a menacing step forward and Stollers shrank back. "Do you know that Lady Beatrice, the woman you just called a whore, is my niece?"

Instant fear filled Stollers' eyes.

"Nay, I did not. Forgive me, my lord." He glanced to Beatrice. "I apologize, my lady. 'Twas a misunderstanding on my part."

She glared at him. "I do not accept your apology." Beatrice raised her chin a notch and looked to her uncle.

"Do you, Edwin Stollers, Baron of Brookhaven, hold my niece's husband, the Baron of Ashcroft, in your dungeons?"

"Her . . . husband?" Fear quickly replaced shock on the nobleman's face. He visibly quaked.

Beatrice did not suppress the smile that came as she looked on with interest.

"I'll see that he's brought to you at once, my lord."

Gilbert looked down at Stollers in disgust. "You're a sniveling coward, Stollers, not fit to lick the boots of your grandfather." His eyes narrowed as his face came close to his enemy's. "Watch your step. If anything you do displeases me, I'll be sure the king hears of it and strips you of everything. I am Edward's man, and I have his ear. And I never make idle threats."

Stollers merely bobbed his head and fled.

Beatrice stepped next to her uncle and laid a hand on his sleeve. "You were magnificent, Uncle. I am proud to call you family."

He threw an arm about her shoulders and gave her a squeeze. "I look forward to meeting this husband of yours. Anyone smart enough to marry my niece is a man to be reckoned with."

RAYNOR SAT ON the damp, chilled ground, his forearms resting on his knees. He'd nearly gone out of his mind at what might be happening above stairs. Beatrice was so small and needed his protection. He worried what Stollers might be capable of. Trying to bribe the guards had come to no avail. They hadn't spoken to him since.

How could he escape this dungeon cell and rescue his wife?

He heard a shuffling noise and came to his feet. Edwin Stollers ventured into his line of sight. He murmured something to the guard closest to him. The soldier retrieved the keys hanging on the wall and slid one into the lock of the cell door. The man turned it and pulled open the door. Raynor stepped out, and the guard slammed it behind him.

Stollers looked a mess. His nose sat crooked on his face and was twice its normal size. Raynor fought the smile that threatened to break out. It seemed his lessons with Beatrice had come to fruition.

"My most profound apology, my lord," Stollers stammered. "I'm sorry for any miscommunication that came between us. You're free to go."

"Did Lady Beatrice break your nose?"

"She did, my lord," he sputtered.

"And did she cause you any other pain?"

Stollers merely nodded.

"Good," Raynor said.

"Your wife... she is waiting for you. Upstairs. With her uncle. You're to join them at once."

Wife? Stollers knew they had married. And... her uncle?

Raynor stared at Stollers until the man finally met his eyes. "Never venture south, Stollers. If you do, I will kill you."

"I... understand, my lord. I promise that you won't catch sight of me as long as you live."

Raynor strode up the stairs without a backward glance. His curiosity built the entire way. He pushed open the heavy door that led to the first floor of the keep and hurried down a passageway toward the great hall.

"Raynor!"

He caught sight of Beatrice, his one true love, the one woman he never wanted to be parted from again.

They ran to each other and Raynor swept her up into his arms. His mouth sought hers in a hungry kiss. Beatrice's arms wound about his neck. He slowly lowered her to her feet, drinking her in, tasting her sweetness, drowning in her scent.

She was the one who broke their kiss. "I love you," she exclaimed and returned her lips to his for another lingering kiss. Beatrice pulled away again. "I have so much to tell you," she said eagerly.

"I already know you broke Stollers' nose."

She beamed. "I did, indeed, my lord husband, and I enjoyed doing so. I also stomped on his foot and kicked him in the groin. You would have been so proud to see me in action."

He rewarded her with a swift kiss. "I would've paid good coin to have seen that, sweetheart." Raynor glanced at the group staring at them. Each man wore a smile on his face. Raynor recognized Sir

Thomas Applegate and Ronald, the soldier from Ashcroft who held Beatrice's lute in his hand, but the third proved unfamiliar to him.

"I hear you are my wife's uncle," he called out. He wrapped an arm about her waist and went to meet the man.

The nobleman thrust out a hand. "I'm Gilbert Lovet and I am Beatrice's uncle. I was brother to her father Richard."

Raynor shook his hand. "Even I have heard of the powerful Earl of Lovet," he said. "I didn't know I'd married into such a lofty family."

"I had no idea, Raynor," Beatrice exclaimed. "After I bashed Stollers around, I rode Fury to seek help and—"

"You rode Fury?" he asked, astonished that she would climb onto the large beast.

"Aye, I did. It felt marvelous."

"She always was a horsewoman. From the time she was three," noted Gilbert, the pride evident in his voice.

"And I caught up to Ronald on the road."

Ronald grinned at him and bowed his head. "My lord. I brought news of your brother."

"Is Peter ill?" Raynor asked, worried why a messenger had been sent such a long way.

"Nay, my lord. He's decided to seek a quieter life in a monastery and renounced the title. *You* are now Baron of Ashcroft, my lord."

The news stunned Raynor. He looked down at a smiling Beatrice.

"Ronald and I came across my uncle and Sir Thomas on the road. He recognized me at the inn where we met."

Applegate said, "She is the spitting image of her mother at that age, my lord. I had no doubt she was Sir Richard and Lady Lucy's missing daughter. And when I heard her name was Beatrice, I knew I must ride to my friend Gilbert and tell him his long-lost niece had finally been found."

"Lucy was mad with grief after my brother's death," Gilbert explained. "She disappeared with Beatrice years ago. From what my niece says, Lucy returned to her father's household. I searched but never found any sign of them. Then Thomas brought me the good news, so I had to seek her out."

"I have a family, Raynor," Beatrice added. "A grandmother and aunt. And cousins!"

She rested her head against his chest. Raynor could feel the happiness radiating from her.

"So you rode my horse. Brought back help in one of the most powerful men of the north, who just happens to be your uncle. And you gained my release." Raynor kissed the top of her head. "I worried that you'd need rescuing but, instead, you have saved me. I'd say you've put in a good day's work, Wife. A very good day."

"Let us depart this foul place," Gilbert said. Raynor caught a hopeful look in the earl's eye. "Might I talk you into stopping at Lovet Castle on your way home? I know you're the new baron and eager to return to your estate, but we'd be pleased to host you and my niece for a few days."

Raynor looked down at the woman who held his heart. "What do you say, my love? Shall we go meet this family of yours?"

Beatrice nodded, tears brimming in her eyes.

"Then let's be off," he said. As the men turned away and headed for the door, Raynor bent to steal one last, precious kiss from his wife, Beatrice, Baroness of Ashcroft. Mother of his future children.

And the love of his life.

"RAYNOR!" BEATRICE EXCLAIMED from the top of the steps that led to the keep. "I was afraid you'd be late. Lord Geoffrey and Lady Merryn will arrive at any moment. Oh, I'm so nervous." She began twisting her wedding ring as she worried her bottom lip.

"I told you I'd return in time to greet them." He raced up the steps and gave her a soft kiss. For a moment, the world stopped as he reveled in the touch of his lips on hers.

"There's no time for kissing," she scolded.

"I always believe there's time for kissing," he replied, stealing another quick one from her. "And you've nothing to fear. You will adore

Geoffrey and Merryn. They are my closest friends."

"But what if they don't like me?"

"What's not to like? You're an intelligent woman, Beatrice Le Roux. One of beauty and passion and charm. My greatest fear is that they'll like you even more than they do me."

She punched his arm good-naturedly. "You tease me, Husband."

Raynor cupped her cheek. "That I do, Wife. But I have something that I believe will give you confidence when you meet my friends."

Her eyes lit with curiosity. "You brought me something?"

"I did, but you need to close your eyes. It's a surprise."

"Raynor!"

"Do not Raynor me. Simply shut your eyes and practice a little patience."

"And if I can't?"

He grinned. "Then I'll take off running. And hope I run faster than you, for if you catch me? You might blacken my eye and bloody my nose. Then what would Geoffrey and Merryn think of you?"

Beatrice pursed her lips. "If Merryn is half the woman you describe, then I'd say she'll approve of me putting you in your place."

Raynor burst out laughing. "You would be right about that. But come, Beatrice. I am serious. Close your eyes, sweetheart."

She did as he asked. He removed the gift from his pocket and went to stand behind her. His arms lifted over her and he fastened the clasp about her neck. Then his fingers slid down her breasts and splayed across her stomach, drawing her into him.

He watched as she looked down. Her hands came up to touch the jewelry. Satisfaction filled him when she gasped. Beatrice wiggled, freeing herself from his grasp. She turned to face him.

Raynor would never forget the look of joy that spread across her lovely face.

"My mother's pearl necklace! However did you get it back?" She fingered the piece again, then rested her palms against his chest. Her large brown eyes met his. Raynor's insides melted.

"I'm a most persuasive man." he quipped. "And this Amfrid fellow wanted to please me more than anything."

"I love you," Beatrice said. "Not only for returning my mother's necklace to me, but for being the man you are each day."

"I love you more," Raynor told her. "With each passing day, my love for you grows."

"Are you two so much in love that you didn't even hear our horses arrive?"

Raynor looked down and saw Geoffrey and Merryn mounting the steps. The two men pounded each other hard on the back in greeting, while Merryn gave Beatrice a warm hug.

"What a lovely necklace," Merryn said.

Beatrice cast a loving smile at him. "There's a story behind it," she confided to Merryn.

Merryn's eyes danced with interest. "I'm sure you have several stories for me." She linked her arm through Beatrice's. "I want to hear everything. How you met. How you fell in love. And in return, I'll tell you a few interesting stories about your husband."

The women started into the keep. As they reached the door, Beatrice looked back over her shoulder and winked at Raynor.

Raynor blew her a kiss as Geoffrey began laughing.

"My cousin—in love and finally married." Geoffrey threw an arm about Raynor's shoulder. "Come on, Baron Le Roux. We have a lot to discuss."

Raynor looked at his best friend. "We do, indeed. It's a story that ends in love. We are lucky men, Geoffrey de Montfort. Lucky men, indeed, for finding the women we have."

They crossed the threshold of Ashcroft, his castle. His home.

One that would always be filled with love.

EPILOGUE

Ashcroft—1382

RAYNOR GAZED DOWN at Beatrice. She'd pushed the bedclothes aside while asleep. He had a wonderful view of the body he'd worshipped for almost twenty years. His palm covered her breast, gently kneading it. She sighed, a contented smile touching her lips. He toyed with the nipple, first with his fingers and then his tongue. Soon, the passion flared between them. Raynor loved how she called out his name. Even after hundreds of times of making love to her, each encounter brought them closer. He would want this woman till he went to the grave—and beyond.

Their love play ended, slow and sweet, as they came together. Raynor thought it was like the music she played for him when they were alone.

"It's hard to believe that today is the day Cecily will be married," Raynor said.

Beatrice's eyes glistened with tears. "It seems only yesterday she was our firstborn."

"Are you sad, sweetheart?"

"No," she assured him. "These are tears of joy. I'm happy for her. William is a good man and he will make a good husband."

Raynor brought her hand to his mouth and kissed it. "But will they love as well as we have?"

Beatrice smiled. "We can only hope they do." She stroked his cheek. "Come. She'll be here soon. We need to dress."

He insisted that he be allowed to brush her hair, still a luscious brown with a few stray strands of gray starting to show. It was one of his favorite things to do. He remembered the broken comb she'd had all those years ago. He'd replaced it with this jeweled one.

A knock sounded at the door and Raynor called, "Come."

Cecily dashed in, her cheeks bright with color. His eldest child looked so much like her mother that Raynor felt as if he'd drawn back a curtain and looked into the past.

"Mother said you wanted to see me," Cecily said.

"Aye," he told her. "We have a gift for you."

"I don't need a gift. You've been the best parents I could ask for. That's been your greatest gift to me."

"Still, we want to give you something on your wedding day to William."

Raynor watched the dreamy smile that turned the corners of Cecily's mouth up. His eyes caught Beatrice's, and they grinned at one another.

Beatrice went to the casket that rested on a low table. She brought out the string of pearls that she'd worn every day since he'd returned them to her right after they had married.

His wife held them up and told their daughter, "My father gave these to my mother on their wedding day. She passed them down to me. I've worn them for many years. Now it's your turn to own them."

Cecily's eyes grew wide. "Mother, I can't! You love your pearls."

Raynor went to stand next to his daughter and rested his hands on her shoulders. "We want you to have them, Cecily." He leaned in and whispered in her ear. When he raised back up, she nodded.

"All right." Cecily went to her mother and offered her back. She raised her hair so that Beatrice could fasten the clasp. Cecily looked down at the necklace and smiled.

"They look lovely against your creamy skin," Beatrice told her. "Now run along to your chamber. I'll come help you dress in a few minutes."

Cecily kissed both of her parents on the cheek and left the room, glowing.

"I think it was the right thing to do," Beatrice said.

"Will you miss wearing them?" Raynor asked.

"A little, but Cecily is our only daughter. I wanted her to have them. We can find something else to give the boys when they wed."

Raynor said, "I also have something for you, my love."

Beatrice looked surprised. "You do?"

He went to his boot and turned it upside down into his palm. He'd hidden her gift inside it, knowing she would never think to look for anything there.

Raynor crossed the room and dangled the pendant from his fingers. "I love how your brown eyes are rimmed in amber. This jewel matches them."

Her lips trembled, fresh tears sprang to her eyes. He placed the pendant around her neck and gave her a soft kiss. Beatrice looked down and touched the stone with reverence.

"I love it and I love you, Raynor Le Roux."

"I love you, Beatrice Le Roux." He offered her his arm. "Let's go see our eldest child marry."

They left the bedchamber where they'd spent so many nights in each other's arms. Raynor knew there would be many more nights of love to come.

The End

About the Author

As a child, Alexa Aston gathered her neighborhood friends together and made up stories for them to act out, her first venture into creating memorable characters. Following her passion for history and love of learning, she became a teacher who began writing on the side to maintain her sanity in a sea of teenage hormones.

Alexa's historical romances use history as a backdrop to place her characters in extraordinary circumstances, where their intense desire for one another grows into the treasured gift of love.

She is the author of *The Knights of Honor*, a medieval romance series that takes place in 14th century England during the reign of Edward III and centers on the de Montfort family. Each romance focuses on the code of chivalry that bound knights of this era.

A native Texan, Alexa lives with her husband in a Dallas suburb, where she eats her fair share of dark chocolate and plots out stories while she walks every morning. She enjoys reading, watching movies and sports, and can't get enough of *Fixer Upper* or *Game of Thrones*. Alexa also writes romantic suspense, western historicals, and standalone medieval novels as Lauren Linwood.

Alexa loves to hear from her readers. You can connect with her through FB, Twitter, and her website, alexaaston.wordpress.com.

Facebook:
www.facebook.com/authoralexaaston

Twitter:
twitter.com/AlexaAston

Amazon Page:
amazon.com/author/alexaaston

Made in the USA
Middletown, DE
20 February 2017